Download My Free Book

If you would like to receive a FREE copy of my psychological thriller 'Just One Second', then you can find the link to the book at my website
www.danielhurstbooks.com

THE RIVALS

DANIEL HURST

www.danielhurstbooks.com

3

PROLOGUE

The crowds of people that had gathered in the town centre to witness feats of both physical and mental endurance had spent most of the morning cheering, clapping and smiling.

But now they were screaming.

The reason for the sudden change in mood was because someone's life was in danger.

No one in the crowd knew who the woman on the floor was, but they did know one thing. She was in trouble, and she needed help immediately.

With so many people around, it would have seemed like that help would have been on hand quickly, but that was not the case. Everybody just seemed to be pointing and staring as if they were too shocked to know what to do, so they could only add to the problem rather than solve it. What this situation needed was for somebody to take charge and bring it back under control.

So why wasn't anybody doing that?

Perhaps it was a case of there simply being too many people around, and in all the chaos and confusion, everybody was waiting for somebody else to make a move. But then there was movement, and it came in the form of the woman wearing the black vest with the white number 577 stuck to the front of it.

Number 577 ran towards the woman on the ground, who was sporting the number 576, and their adjoining numbers suggested they had signed up to this marathon at the same time.

Did that mean they were friends?

Was this woman going to help?

Everybody in the crowd certainly hoped so, at least until a trained medical professional could get here and administer aid. But then those in attendance saw that help had not arrived in the form of 577.

She had stopped, and she was standing over the stricken woman, but she didn't look worried, or desperate, or like she was about to try administering some sloppy version of CPR.

She looked quite happy.

The crowd knew that because the woman was smiling.

She was smiling while the woman at her feet lay dying.

BEFORE

1

LUCY

I open one eye and stare at the digital clock on the bedside table that has stirred me from my slumber. The incessant beeping coming from it would be enough to drag anyone out of the dream world and back into the real one, and it's a relief when I hit the button and stop the alarm. It's also a relief when I close my one open eye again and return to complete darkness, even though I know doing so is to play a very risky game called 'falling back to sleep.'

I should open my eyes. I should get up. And I should get out the front door.

It's 05:00. My one-eye glance at the alarm clock told me that, which means it is time for me to leave the warmth and comfort of my duvet behind and head out onto the cold, wet streets of my hometown so that I can log another 10k run before another day's work. Of course, I don't have to do it. I could just roll over and go back to sleep, and every single sinew in my body is screaming at me to do just that.

You're tired. You work too hard. You deserve a lie-in today.

The words my fuzzy, sleep-deprived brain is telling me are all very nice and comforting, but they aren't very helpful when it comes to hitting my goals. That's why I pull back the duvet without another moment's thought, exposing myself to the freezing air in the flat that I share with my friend, Kirsty, before getting off the bed and scampering around in the dark to put on my clothes as quickly as possible.

I know that my flatmate will be sleeping soundly in the adjoining bedroom, unless my alarm clock woke her too, which it has been known to do on occasion. Kirsty is usually a lively, positive soul but not so much when she gets woken up at the crack of dawn by me, so I could only apologise for waking her in the past and promise her I would do better to be quiet in the future. That's why I'm trying so hard not to make a noise now as I creep from my bedroom to the bathroom after quickly dressing in my running gear that I'd strategically left outside my wardrobe so I could find it easier in the low lighting.

Flicking the switch for the bathroom light is always one of the hardest parts of my morning, and this time is no different as I screw up my face and try not to be blinded by the dazzling beam from the bulb above my head. It takes a few moments for my eyes to adjust before I go over to the sink and look at my reflection in the mirror. As always, I'm a mess. There are bags under my eyes, my skin looks red and blotchy, and my dark hair has the same style as it would have if I had stuck my head in a washing machine. I let out a big yawn then for good measure to really round out 'my look.'

Thankfully, I don't always look like this. This is my 'just got out of bed' look or what I like to refer to sometimes as 'Dawn Diva.' It can be a little frightening for me or any man I might share my bed with from time to time, but it's nothing that a shower, some make-up

11

and a hairdryer can't sort out. But right now, I'm not interested in beautifying myself, nor do I have any time to do such a thing even if I wanted to.

I just need to do what I have to do in here and then get out of the house.

I complete my bathroom necessities quickly and quietly, neglecting to flush the toilet but only because that's another thing that has been known to wake Kirsty up in the past. I'll flush it when I get back in around an hour or so because it will be a more suitable hour of the day then and Kirsty should have started to wake anyway.

Leaving the bathroom, I creep down the hallway, skilfully avoiding any creaky floorboards that are yet another thing that have caused Kirsty to emerge from her room before sunrise and grumble at me for being the worst flatmate in the world. I know I'm not the worst flatmate in the world, and I'm sure that Kirsty knows it too, but 5 o'clock in the morning is not a time for sensible conversation and considered thought. For Kirsty, it's a time for sleep and nothing else, which explains why she can erupt so explosively if that sleep is interrupted by me moving around our home. But I manage to make it to the front door without making a sound, and as I put on my trainers, I get that little jitter of excitement that always washes over me at this point.

This is the last day of a ten-day challenge that I have been taking part in, and it's always at this part that I feel the familiar wave of nerves and eager anticipation that comes when I'm seconds away from doing what I do best.

Competing.

I'm thirty-five, but I've always loved to pit myself against someone else ever since I can remember. I have no siblings, which meant I didn't get my childhood competition as easily as others at that age, but that just meant I had to set my sights on bigger foes, and they came in the form of my parents, mainly.

I would always try and compete with my mum and dad and always, always try to win. Whether it was playing a board game or something more active in the back garden, I would hustle and focus like my life depended on it, wanting to come out victorious and not being satisfied unless I had. Of course, being a small child meant it wasn't easy for me to defeat adults at certain games, or at least it shouldn't have been, except my parents were the sweet kind who usually gave me an advantage by not trying as hard as they could. That meant I got more than my fair share of wins growing up, but that joy only lasted until I was old enough to realise that they were going easy on me. That was the point when I knew I needed to find better opposition who didn't love me so much that they conceded defeat so easily.

My classmates at school provided that next opposition, and it's amazing how the education system can be such a playground for those who like to measure themselves against others. Whether it be the result of a Maths test or the results of an egg and spoon race on Sports Day, I found school to be the perfect place for me to get my competitive juices flowing and give me my daily fix of trying to win.

But unlike at home where I was winning regularly, I didn't have things all my own way at school. That's because everyone was my age and at my level, both physically and mentally, and that made it a level playing field. It was fertile ground for a fair fight. The challenge was to get ahead in that kind of environment.

And get ahead, I did.

The drive that saw me study more for exams and perfect balancing an egg on a spoon while everyone else at school was watching cartoons and annoying their parents is the same drive that is motivating me to leave my flat now and go out onto these empty streets. It's the drive to get better and the drive to prove it by having tangible results to point to.

Looking down at my phone, I see the app that shows how I have been faring so far in this ten-day challenge, but more importantly, I see how the other people taking part in it have been faring too. Times. Rankings. *Leader boards.* I love all those things because that's how I get to measure myself against others and determine whether or not I am winning. And I can clearly see on this app that I am winning right now.

I've not missed a day of this challenge so far because doing so would mean elimination, and the times I have been recording have been enough to put me at the top of this virtual leader board, above all these other people who I will never meet but share a strange bond with, nonetheless. It's the bond that says we all need this competitive element in our lives to get us out of bed in the morning and fuel our days.

Don't get me wrong, I'm not just some obsessive competitor with nothing else to my life. I have a normal job and a few friends, and I put my feet up from time to time when I feel like I deserve it, watching TV and eating snacks like everybody else at the end of a long day. But I'm not going to deny that I like to compete. And as long as there is somebody out there who fancies a challenge, then I will be up for it.

Fortunately, there always is, which is why as I set off running to wrap up my current challenge, I have a big smile on my face because I'm already looking forward to the next one.

2

JESS

I can see the sun cresting on the horizon as I look out of my kitchen window with bleary eyes, and the glow of yellow light gives me the boost of optimism I need to finish my work. Looking back down at the plate in front of me, I see the scrambled eggs, the avocado and the granary bread, and it looks appetising. I'd love nothing more than to take a knife and fork and scoop some of this food into my mouth, and I know my rumbling stomach wants me to do that too.

But this meal wasn't made to be eaten.

It was made to be showcased.

I take a photo of the plate before taking several more, experimenting with angles and light and anything else I can think of that will give my image the best chance to dazzle. Then, when I think I have it, I decide the moment of truth has arrived. It's time to upload my effort to the internet, where it will be judged and where a winner will be announced.

This 'Beautiful Breakfast' competition is just one of the many that run on a daily basis on the app I have on my phone that allows me to get my competitive juices flowing in an easy way. This competition is also the reason I am up so early because producing a breakfast that stands a chance of being deemed the winner requires a lot of time and effort. That's why my alarm went off at 04:30 and it's why it has taken me over an hour of cooking to get something on the plate that I am proud of.

An outside observer could say that I have wasted a lot of time, food and money this morning, and my bin is certainly full enough to prove that thanks to all the eggs, avocado and burnt toast I have tossed away during my pursuit of the best breakfast. But I just see all of that as necessary because, in order to win, one has to be prepared to make sacrifices and take risks.

The sacrifice has come in losing out on sleep and also losing out on a lot of food that was good enough to eat but not good looking enough to be entered into a competition. The risk comes in that I could have gone to all that trouble for nothing, and my photo might not get any votes, rendering this whole thing a waste of time because winning is all that matters to someone like me.

As a high-flying saleswoman for an international, award-winning office design company, competing and winning is not just fun but how I pay for food, clothing and the roof above my head. While this breakfast game might not be as serious as what I do for employment, it is still linked in that trying to win here is the reason I am able to win in the workplace. It requires all the same skills, disciplines and traits, except it's just in a different arena. The office is where I compete for money, but this app is where I compete for fun, and make no mistake, this is a lot of fun to me.

I'm not the only one who feels this way if the number of users on this app is anything to go by. At last count, there were over two million users on here in the

UK, and five thousand of those are in my hometown. I never meet any of these people because that's not the point of it. We're here to challenge ourselves, not make friends, and there's no challenge without somebody else to be measured against.

Right now, I am measuring myself against the forty-five other people who have entered this breakfast game today.

With my entry already submitted, I just have to wait to see who the 'Judge' picks as the best one. That judge is a randomly assigned person who will be fair and proper, two qualities that might be welcomed in a contest like this but are not necessarily helpful in the real world where people will do anything to get ahead.

I didn't get to be the top-performing saleswoman at work for the last three years without crossing a few lines and taking a few risks, risks that some of my colleagues do not have the guts to take. But all I care about is getting results and, most of all, getting the best result.

Whoever said 'it's not the winning that counts but the taking part' would not have lasted two seconds around me.

The brilliant sunrise is working wonders on helping me pass the time before the winner of this latest competition gets announced, but it's not distracting me entirely, so I scroll through the app to see what other people are up to on there this morning. I see there is a contest underway for 'Best Fancy Dress Costume', as well as a 'Best Magic Trick' and 'Best Life Hack.' There's also a '10k for 10 Days' challenge underway that I almost participated in myself but decided against at the last minute because I have a lot on at work at the moment and can't commit to such a big contest.

And if I can't commit, then I can't expect to win.

I could spend hours looking at all the different competitions that have either started or are coming up, as well as clicking on the profiles of all the potential rivals I could have if I engaged them in contest, but I don't have hours. I need to start getting ready for work while keeping one eye on the results of the breakfast challenge.

I'm so wrapped up in the prospect of winning my eleventh competition since I signed up to the app that I've completely forgotten to eat the food I put on my plate, and by the time I remember, it's stone cold. I pick at it with my fork for a moment before deciding that I'll just throw it away and grab something on the way into the office, which won't be too much of a hassle for me. There's a great café on the way, and I like going in there when I can because the owner runs a reward system for regular customers. Whoever gets the most stamps on their coffee card per month wins a free lunch, and just like everything else in my life, I like to win that particular contest as often as I can.

After showering and dressing, I'm all set to leave, and the sun has fully risen as I close and lock my front door before making my way to my car. But just before I start the engine, I hear the notification on my phone, and it's a noise that I recognise and respond to. Just like Pavlov trained his dog to salivate at the sound of a bell because the animal associated it with mealtimes, this notification stimulates a response from me. It's excitement mixed in with a little bit of anxiety.

I'm excited because another competition has just ended.

And I'm anxious because I'm not sure if I have won yet.

Opening the app, I nervously nibble on my lower lip as I check the results of the 'Best Breakfast' contest. But when I see them, I stop nibbling and start smiling.

I've done it again.

I've won.

'Get in!' I cry out loud before giving a little fist pump for good measure. Sure, it's not the biggest victory in my life, but it's still a win, and they all count, no matter how small. It might seem like a childish thing for an almost forty-year-old woman to do, but this is me, and I'm not going to apologise for who I am. That's because I am a very successful businesswoman sitting in a nice car on the way to go and do a job that rewards me for being fiery and ambitious. Other women my age might be busying themselves with their children, getting them dressed and out the door for the school run, or on their way to work daydreaming about last night's reality show and how many weeks it is now until their next holiday.

But that's not me. I'm different to them.

I'm different to them all.

I am a machine - an unapologetic, motivated, winning machine, and I will beat them all at any game they want to play. The only problem I have is finding enough people to play with me, or rather, challenge me. I'm dominating my colleagues in the workplace, and I'm dominating everyone I come up against on this app. I guess that's because most people just play for fun. But life isn't just some game to be taken lightly. It's all or nothing.

Forget win or learn, to me it's win or perish.

As I start driving, tapping the steering wheel and singing along to the song on the radio, buoyant after yet another victory, I am happy. But this will just be a fleeting feeling. It's only a matter of time until my insatiable appetite for defeating an opponent rears its head again.

That never changes, and I guess at this age, it never will.

That's fine by me.

3

LUCY

Some offices are not known for being dynamic places where the employees are constantly stimulated. In fact, most workplaces get by thanks to caffeination rather than motivation. But I'm pleased to say that my workplace is not one of those. At this recruitment agency, everybody who walks through the door not only knows what is expected of them, but they expect it of themselves too.

I love my job, which I appreciate is a rare thing to be able to say, so I don't take it for granted. But I've been working here for eight years, and in all that time, I've hardly ever had a bad day. Sure, I've had days where I was tired, or frustrated, or just irritated by the sound of one of my colleague's voices, but which office worker doesn't get like that from time to time?

But the main reason I like it here is because it's the perfect environment for a person like me.

Being a competitive soul has led to me achieving a lot, but I'm also aware that it can be a little intimidating for other people who aren't as like-minded. Not everybody wants to get up and go running at dawn, nor do they feel as though they are in constant competition with themselves or others. I understand that, and occasionally, I am a little jealous of it too.

Take Kirsty, my flatmate, for example. She is like me in many ways, which is why we are friends, but one area in which we differ greatly is how we view competition. Kirsty has no interest in trying to beat other people, whether it be in her family, her workplace, at the gym, or on an app on a mobile phone. She wouldn't care if she came last in a race, nor would she lose a single second of sleep if she discovered that there was somebody out there who could do something better than she could do it. She would just get on with her life in a blissful state, only pausing sometimes to chuckle at those who are like me and feel the need to compete.

While I was running in cross-country races at school, Kirsty was the classmate who was dawdling at the back, more interested in having a laugh and avoiding the glare of a teacher than trying to win and secure the prestige that came with it. Perhaps that is the main reason we became friends and have stayed so close over the years. It's because she is one of the few people in my life I have never felt in competition with. Because of that, she's the only one I can ever truly relax around.

There's certainly no time for relaxing here in this busy office on a midweek morning, not when there are sales targets to hit and bonuses to be handed out. All the desk spaces are occupied, and all the occupants are either making phone calls or replying to emails. It's organised chaos, but every single action is done with one intention, and that is to win. We're trying to win for our clients, our employer, and, of course, ourselves.

As a recruitment consultant, my job is to place candidates with prospective employers. But contrary to popular belief, it's not an easy job in which we simply have to send a few applicants to an office for an interview. The real key to success in this industry is to be able to drum up business yourself. That means instead of waiting for a company to phone and ask if I know someone who might be a good fit for their latest role, I phone them and find the openings before they even exist. That's only possible by building good relationships with them because I'm not the only recruitment consultant in this town, and there's plenty of competition in this industry as everybody vies to get the most business. But I've been doing this long enough now to have not only figured out what works best for me but also what works best for everyone else I come into contact with on a daily basis.

I like to start my working day by ringing around some of my best clients and asking them how things are going. Personal stuff like how their kids are doing, or what they have planned for the weekend, or where they are thinking of going on holiday next. Then, after ten minutes of almost making them forget that they are at work, I get to work myself. I find out if they are looking to fill any roles, particularly if they haven't got around to advertising them yet, and if so, I assure them that they only need to use me to fill that role and no one else. Getting work this way means there is less chance that it goes to my competition, and it also means my boss is extremely pleased with the results I give him, and in this type of work, a happy boss means one thing.

A good bonus.

I depend on bonuses because my basic wage isn't great here, despite how long I've done this job and how good I am at it. It's still mostly commission, like anything else to do with sales, so those bonuses are the things that can really ramp up my income. But I don't seek them because I have an urge to make lots of money and buy better things for myself. I seek them simply because getting a bonus means I've done a good job.

But I'm not going to lie, having more money would help. That's because it would be nice to own my own place one day instead of sharing a flat with my friend. I love having a flatmate, and I love how we get to spend most nights laughing together on the sofa with a bottle of wine and a rom-com on the TV, but I'm aware it's not going to last forever. Kirsty is going to want her own place one day too because I know she wants to find a good man, get married, and have lots of babies. When that day comes, I'll have two choices.

Find a new flatmate. Or get a place on my own.

There's no way I'll ever be able to replace Kirsty as a perfect living companion, so I wouldn't even bother trying. I'd just get my own place but to do that, I need as much money as possible. Of course, I could find myself my own guy to share the cost with, but that would mean actually going on a date, and I haven't been on one of them in years. I have no one to blame for that but myself because I know why my earlier relationships failed, and it's the same reason why I'm so reluctant to try and get into another one.

It's my competitive nature.

It's really not compatible with a healthy relationship.

Instead of being at ease with my previous boyfriends and letting them know all my vulnerabilities,

25

I was always trying to out-do them. I had to be the best cook out of the two of us, or the highest earner, or the one who told the best story about their day. I know that's ridiculous, and plenty of my exes told me so too, but that's just the way it was. I guess I'll have to figure out my issues with that someday unless I want to spend my life alone while all my friends marry and have kids, but at this time of my life, my competitive streak is serving me well. I'm killing it at work and enjoying every second of it. I'm also enjoying the fact that the app on my phone has just told me that I was the best performer in the '10k in 10 Days' challenge. According to their stats, my average running time was better than the other participants, so while they completed the challenge the same as me, I was the one who did it best.

It's another happy moment for me.

And then I pick up the phone and call my next client because life goes on, and there's always another race to run.

4

JESS

I notice the woman sitting in the reception area of this glitzy office in an affluent part of this town the second I walk through the revolving doors. It's Mary, my business rival, who works for a competitor of my employer and, therefore, is always popping up in the same places as me. She is out here trying to secure business with the same clients that I am because we do the same job, and because of that, we've seen plenty of each other over the years. But despite our history, neither of us bother with things like small talk. We barely even acknowledge each other's presence, and I do nothing to change that fact as I inform the receptionist that I am here for my appointment and then take a seat opposite Mary on one of the plush leather sofas.

I can sense my rival's eyes on me as I check my phone, but I don't look up, not interested in making eye contact because to do so would be to let her know that she has entered my realm of consciousness, and I'm not even prepared to give her that. But then she speaks to me, and despite not wanting to engage with her, I kind of have to now.

'Excuse me?' I say, looking up from my phone.

'I was just asking you what time your appointment is?'

'Half-past one. You?'

'One o'clock. You're very early then.'

'I'm always early. It sets a good example.'

'Perhaps. But I'm first, and sometimes that is all that counts.'

The door behind reception opens a second later, before I can reply to Mary's last statement, and when it does, I see the man we are both here to visit step out and give us a smile. Then he lets Mary know that he is ready for their meeting before she gets up and follows him. But just before she disappears from view, she makes sure to turn back and give me a smile, her way of reinforcing what she just said to me about her being first.

I make sure not to let her see how much she is annoying me as she goes through the door, but inside I am burning with motivation. I want to beat her, as I always do, but even more so now after what she just said to me. Being first does count, which was why I tried to get this meeting earlier. But this was the only time the client could fit me in, and I see Mary was able to squeeze herself in before me. Now she is the one getting to give her sales pitch while I'm sat out here waiting my turn.

We're both here to convince the owner of this office that he should use our company for the renovation project they have planned. The interior and exterior of this building are due to be revamped, and it's a million-pound job for whichever company is awarded the contract. I'm here today to secure those million pounds for my boss, but Mary is here to do the same for hers, and only one of us will win.

I find myself fidgeting as I wait for that door to open again, all the while my mind wondering with thoughts of what Mary could be saying as she tries to beat me. I know that I'm better than her at this job, and my track record proves it, but every time we cross paths, it is a new challenge, and that's why I can't ever relax and give her a chance.

It's twenty-five minutes later when I see my rival reappear, and when I do, I see that she has a big smile on her face. The man she has just been talking to is also smiling, so I guess that means their meeting has gone well. I'm not at a disadvantage because I'm going second, and Mary knows it as she wishes me 'good luck' on her way through reception and out of the building. But I just grit my teeth and silently urge myself on as I stand and prepare to go into battle.

Come on, Jess. You've got this.

My meeting begins with me accepting the warm greeting from David, the man I am here to impress, before he shows me around some of the bigger rooms in this office that he has grand plans for. While it's a fairly basic environment now that looks as dated as every one of the fifty years it has been standing for, the budget he has at his disposal means that very soon, this building will be brought into the modern age. David wants a gym here, as well as a games room and a huge kitchen for staff to be able to unwind in. He also wants to completely alter the seating plan and allow for more space for more desks as his company grows in the future. But the main thing he wants to do is take advantage of the incredible views this office has from the upper floors, and that's where we are now, standing in the current boardroom as we discuss his plans for the new boardroom.

'I'd like the table to be facing out this way so that potential clients can really get the full impact of the view while we have our meetings,' David says.

'Of course. That's something my team can help you design. We've just done the Arnott's office down on Serpentine Street, and they have a view not too dissimilar to this one that they wanted to maximise.'

'I understand, but with all due respect, we are bigger than Arnott's, and we want our office to be better than theirs.'

'I know that, and rest assured, if you award us this contract, it will be better.'

David gives nothing away in his facial expression as he invites me to take a seat, and as I sit and take out the brochure that I plan to talk him through, I still don't know what he is thinking.

Is he liking what I am telling him and planning to work with me? Or is he leaning towards choosing Mary and her employer instead?

Whenever I'm in a competition, I like to know where I stand so that way, I know what I still need to do to win. That's why I like the app. It gives me live standings, so I know if I'm ahead or behind and have time to recalibrate if need be. But in this environment, I don't have that. I could be winning, but I could just as easily be losing. Seeing as losing is never an option for me, I need to step my game up a little bit here, and a moment later, David gives me the perfect opportunity to do so.

'So, why should I go with you and not the last woman to sit there?' he asks me as he leans back in his chair with his hands folded across his sizeable stomach, very much in the position of power in this dynamic.

'Well, I could tell you more about how my employer has a bigger turnover, better track record and more experience in this type of job, but you already know that, so I won't bother wasting your time,' I say, beginning confidently but only just getting warmed up. 'Instead, I will tell you something you don't know.'

'Oh, really? And what is that?'

'Mary, the woman who was in here before me? She is good, and don't get me wrong, I'm sure her employer would do just fine if they were to renovate your office for you.'

'Okay, so why wouldn't I choose them? They are slightly cheaper than you, after all.'

'You won't pick them because they're not better than us. And how do I prove that? Well, what if I told you Mary applied for a job at my place recently. Now, why would she do that if she was already working at the better company?'

David thinks about that for a moment, but I don't give him too long to come up with a reply before I press on.

'I'm not going to bother boring you with too many details about why Mary was not taken on by my employer because this isn't about her and her talents. It's about our employers, and the fact that she's good enough to work for them but not for us says a lot. Don't you think?'

'Perhaps.'

'Let me put it this way. I'm not planning on applying for a job at her company anytime soon. That's because I already know that I'm at the best place in town. If you pick us, you will know that too.'

David nods his head and seems impressed with what I have just said. That's why I choose not to say anything more. What else is there to say? If he doesn't go for us after that then he's a fool.

'I'll speak to my legal team about getting contracts drawn up. But for now, take this as my notice that I intend to go with you on this project.'

David extends a hand out to me over the table, and I reach across and accept it, smiling as I lock eyes with him and revel in the feeling of yet another win.

As I stand to leave and take one last look at the spectacular view from this boardroom, I bask in the familiarity of victory. Feeling this way is addictive, and I'll never get enough of it. I'll also always make sure that I do whatever it takes to keep experiencing it. Like lying, for example.

Mary never applied for a job with my employer. I just said that to make myself look better and make her look worse. It was fiction, a story to tip the power balance between us in my favour. She might have been here first, but I have made sure that I am the one who made the lasting impression.

Do I feel guilty for winning in an unsportsmanlike manner?

No, because guilt is for losers.

Winners just smile before focusing on defeating their next opponent.

5

LUCY

It's been a long day, but then I guess any day that begins with a 5am wake-up call will feel long. But now it's the evening, and I'm unwinding as I like to do on the sofa with a glass of wine, a film on the TV, and in the company of my best friend.

Our watching of the film has been interspersed with snippets of conversation as we discuss our day, and that's fine because it's not the kind of movie that demands a viewer's full attention. In fact, it wouldn't be a lie to say it's extremely trashy, and anybody with half a brain cell could have come up with a better plot.

Maybe I should get into movie-making. I could surely come up with something better than this. I also hear it's a very competitive and cut-throat world, especially in Hollywood, and that appeals.

On second thoughts, I think I've got enough on my plate.

'Did I tell you I got the best time in the 10k in 10 Days Challenge?' I ask Kirsty before taking another sip of my wine.

'No, but well done,' she replies with a genuine smile because she knows how much these things mean to me. 'Is that it finished now?'

'Yeah, that's the ten days over with. Can you believe it? It went so fast!'

'So does that mean I don't have to hear your alarm going at five every day now?'

'Oh God, did you hear it today?'

'Yep.'

'I'm sorry, I thought I'd turned it off quickly enough.'

'Not quite. But it's okay. I'll sleep when I'm dead.'

I laugh at my friend's deadpan statement whilst feeling guilty for disturbing her slumber again.

'I'm sorry. I really was trying to be quiet.'

'It's fine. I'm just teasing you. Besides, I'm used to it by now. It's one of the many perks of living with you.'

'There are many perks, I'll give you that.'

I clink my glass against Kirsty's, and we laugh before losing ourselves in the lame movie for the next couple of minutes. By then, I've finished my drink, and I ask my friend if she would like me to get more wine from the kitchen so we can have a second glass.

'Don't worry, I'll go,' she says as she gets off the sofa without giving me any chance to go first. It's not like her to be so keen to go to the fridge, but when she returns, I realise why she is being so nice.

'Would it be possible if I could have the flat to myself tomorrow night until around ten?' Kirsty asks me tentatively after refilling my glass.

'Why?'

'I might have a date.'

'Really? Who with?'

'That guy I went out with last week.'

'I didn't realise you were seeing him again. I thought you said it didn't go well.'

'It wasn't that bad.'

'Obviously not if you're inviting him around here.'

'I know it's short notice, but I would really appreciate if you could make yourself scarce.'

I let out a sigh before thinking about what I could do tomorrow night while Kirsty has her latest love interest over to the flat. I could message another friend and see if they fancy a meet-up, but the problem with that is I don't have too many other friends, or at least none who would be likely to respond positively to such an invite. I could always go and do some late-night shopping, or maybe I could catch a movie at the local cinema. There's nothing I particularly need to buy for myself, nor are there any new films I am desperate to see, but I need to do something because I'm obviously not wanted here.

'Sure. No problem,' I say with a shrug, even if it is a problem. 'I'll find something to keep me out of trouble.'

'Great. Thank you! I owe you one.'

Kirsty seems genuinely thrilled, and even though I now have the headache of filling my evening tomorrow night, I am pleased for her and this guy she obviously likes enough to want to see again.

'So, what have you got planned with lover boy?' I ask her.

'We're just going to get a takeaway and watch a film,' she replies, doing her best to sound casual about it.

'Ahhh, the old takeaway and a movie date. I see. So, what time do you think the pair of you will have finished having sex?'

'Stop it! That's not what we're going to be doing!'

'Hey, I'm a big girl, you don't have to be coy with me.'

'I'm not. It's just a date.'

'Yeah, a date within a few feet of your bed. Very wise.'

Kirsty laughs at my joke, and I laugh too, although part of me does feel a little envious that she might be getting some action and I won't be, even if it is my fault on that front because I'm not exactly receptive to any man's advances these days.

It's almost as if Kirsty reads my mind because she then asks me how my love life is going.

'You know me, mate, I would marry myself if I could,' I tell my friend, hoping a little bit of jesting will help us move on from this topic. But it doesn't work, and Kirsty tries again.

'There's a guy in my office that I think would be perfect for you,' she tells me. 'He's really into sport, and he's always running marathons for charity and trying to beat his personal best time. I figure you and him would get along, what with you both being so active and competitive and such.'

'He sounds nice,' I say with absolutely no enthusiasm in my voice, which only makes Kirsty laugh again.

'Come on, I can give him your number if you'd like. What have you got to lose?'

'I appreciate the offer, but it won't work.'

'Why not? He's almost like the male version of you.'

'Why? Just because he likes competition?'

'Yeah, exactly!'

'That's why it wouldn't work! We'd drive each other mad competing against each other!'

'But I thought that's what you wanted. You always say you can't stand someone who isn't like that!'

'Yeah, I don't want anyone completely different to me. But I don't want anyone too similar either.'

'Then what do you want?'

'I have absolutely no idea.'

I chuckle after my honest confession, and Kirsty rolls her eyes before giving up and going back to the movie. I'm glad she isn't going to push me on this any further because this subject always makes me feel uncomfortable. I am happy being by myself. I don't need a guy. One day I will. But not yet.

Deciding to busy my mind with something else, I take out my phone and go onto my favourite app again. Looking for a new challenge to get my competitive juices flowing now that my last challenge is over, I browse various categories looking for anything that piques my interest. I'm not quite sure what I fancy doing now. A bake-off? An art contest? A memory challenge? I consider all the options, and on this app, there are certainly plenty of them, but after my recent endeavours with the running, I decide I would quite like to do something in the fitness realm again, so I click the 'Exercise' tab and see what there is in there.

The first thing that pops up is a 'Step Challenge', and when I click it, I see that another user is looking for somebody on here to compete against. The challenge is to see who can do the most steps in the next week, and there are no limits or particular targets. It's just a straight walk-off to decide a winner.

I like the sound of it because it will give me an excuse to get out and walk on my lunch hours instead of wasting time in the staff room, so I click the 'Enter' button, and then I get the notification that tells me the challenge is on and it will begin tomorrow.

I think about telling Kirsty what my next fun challenge will be but decide not to as she seems surprisingly engrossed in the film for some reason. But I do check out the details of the person I will be competing against by clicking on their name and accessing their profile.

It's a user called Jess, and she is a little older than me if her bio is to be believed, which isn't always the case because people online like to tell fibs. This could be a sixty-year-old man for all I know, and he just pretends to be a thirty-nine-year-old woman on here. There is a photo of Jess, and she looks pretty, but again, it could be fake. But it doesn't really matter. All I needed was to find somebody to compete against again, and now I have that.

But just before I leave Jess's profile, there is one thing that catches my eye. Her bio lists her location as the same town that I'm in. It's unusual to end up competing against somebody so close because this app could pit me against anyone in the world, but I guess this will be a domestic duel.

Putting my phone down and going back to watching the movie, I try and concentrate on the weak plot and bad acting. But it's no good. Now that I have another challenge to participate in, all I can think about is beating the person I am up against.

Bring it on, Jess.

I hope you give it your best.

I certainly will.

6

JESS

It's a cold, clear morning, and there isn't a cloud in the sky. The birds are tweeting in the trees after being woken by the rising sun, and the sound of car engines is getting louder as more and more commuters come out of their houses and get into their car to get involved in 'rush hour.' This is typically a stressful time as everybody fights to get to their workplace before their deadline, but not for me. That's because I'm walking, and I'm going to be early to work today.

No stress for me.

Just some good, clean fun in the way of a little healthy competition.

I'm currently competing against the user who accepted my challenge on the app last night. Her name is Lucy, and now we are head to head, each of us trying to get more steps in this week than the other. I have no idea who Lucy is, nor do I particularly care. She's just another person for me to beat, and beat her I will.

I would always be confident, but I'm even more so now because a quick check on our current 'Challenge Stats' shows me that she hasn't even started walking yet. The game began at midnight, and while she has obviously been sleeping for most of that time since then, I was half-expecting her to get up early and get that step count ticking over. But it is still showing a big fat zero at her end, so I guess she's still in bed. Meanwhile, my step count is at 3,000 and rising fast as I continue on my way into the office.

I'm walking at a brisk pace, feeling light and free, but it's not just because I'm enjoying the fact that I'm already getting a head start on my opponent. It's because today is the day of the monthly sales meeting, and that's when the latest round of bonuses get announced. Having had my best month ever, I'm expecting the meeting to be a very lucrative one for me. I'm also expecting to get plenty of praise heaped upon me by all my superiors, who always like to hold me up as some kind of shining example of what the other people in my workplace should strive to be like.

I always try and play down the praise, doing my best to be modest because no one likes a bragger, but secretly, I revel in the admiration and respect that I get afforded for doing such a good job. A lot of hard work has gone into making this month's sales figures look so good, but they will be looking even better once David, the owner of the office I visited yesterday, signs on the dotted line. I've already got a verbal agreement from him, and it's just a matter of time until he makes it official, and when he does, that will be seven figures going into the account of my employer, which will result in a healthy amount of money being funnelled into mine in the form of another bonus.

Sometimes, I think about starting my own company where I could sell on behalf of others because then I would take a bigger share of all the profits I am generating, but while that's something I am sure I will get around to doing one day, it's not urgent. I'm making a good living, and it's fun to be the highest performer in a team when others are trying to outperform me. If I become the boss, then it's kind of accepting that I've made it, and no one will overtake me then, and I know I will miss the challenge of having people on the same level as me who think they have a chance at beating me.

I hear a couple of car horns blaring as I turn a corner and walk onto another street, one that's just as busy as the last, but I saunter on past all the heavy traffic and the frustrated faces in the vehicles, my step counter purring away in my pocket as I go. Some people might say that being as competitive as I am is unhealthy, but it feels pretty healthy to me. Look at all this walking I'm doing because I'm motivated by a contest. If I was lacking a challenge then I might just be driving to work now, and that is surely an unhealthier way of travelling.

I wonder what time my opponent, Lucy, is going to get up and get moving. I really hope she isn't going to be one of those challengers that fails to put up a fight and has me bored with how easily I beat her. There's nothing worse than people like that, but, unfortunately, I've had my fair share of those kinds since I started using the app. There was the time when I accepted a user's week-long challenge in which the pair of us had to film ourselves going up to a stranger every day and telling them a joke. The winner would be the one who got the biggest laugh at least four days out of the seven. But it became apparent by day three that my opponent was not witty at all, and her jokes were so lame that I knew I would win easily. It's not as if I'm some hilarious comedian, but I did put a little bit of effort into finding

43

some funny things on the internet, so it's a shame that she didn't bother to do the same. I liked that game because it was a fun challenge to approach a stranger, but while I won, the real fun comes when I know that my opponent did everything they could but they just weren't good enough.

That woman didn't do everything she could to win.

I really hope Lucy is not like that.

As I keep walking, I think about how I've been tempted a couple of times to message one of my challengers on the app and suggest a meet-up. I'd love to meet some more like-minded people, and I presume the app I use is full of them; otherwise, why would they be on there? But most of the people I get pitted against are not in my area, and I'm not bothered enough to travel far just to maybe make a new friend. But according to her profile, Lucy is in the same town as me, so if she proves to be a worthy opponent, then I might just have to send her a message and suggest a drink. I guess it would be an experience if nothing else, and we wouldn't have to meet again if it turned out to be a disaster. But it remains to be seen whether she will give me a good challenge, and on the evidence so far, she isn't going to do that.

My office comes into view ten minutes later, and by the time I reach the steps that lead up to the front door, I skip up them, feeling positively optimistic about what I have already done today and what is still to come. I feel even better when I get inside and see my boss in the lift that takes us up to the fifth floor because while he doesn't go into any specific detail regarding the bonus I am hoping to hear about later, he does tell me to do one thing.

He tells me to be prepared because it's going to be a big one. Then he gives me a wink and walks out of the lift ahead of me, leaving me buzzing with anticipation for the meeting later today.

I keep the smile on my face as I walk past the desk of my other colleagues, none of whom are actually in the office yet because I'm early and they are not as keen as me. Is it any wonder my bonus is going to dwarf theirs later? No, not at all. I work harder than them, and I'm better than them, which is why I'll be the one reaping the biggest rewards.

Sinking down into my leather desk chair, I feel ready to log on and begin another busy day of sending emails before the various meetings I have to attend begin. But just before I do, I make another quick check on the app to see if there has been any progress at Lucy's end. When I do, I see that she has just made forty-seven steps. I wonder if that is just her walking from her bed to the bathroom. Whatever it is, it's nothing compared to my step count, which now stands at a lofty 4,983.

Good luck beating me this week, Lucy.

You're clearly going to need it.

7

LUCY

My eyes are fixed firmly on the clock on my computer screen as I count down to what would be an acceptable time to leave the office and go on my lunch break. I don't always take breaks in my job because I prefer to keep working and keep making great strides in my career, but this week will be different. This week will see me spending every single second of the permitted sixty-minute break away from my desk and out of the office, and I'll be doing one thing and one thing only during that time.

Walking.

A lot.

It was a surprise to see Jess's step tally when I woke up this morning and checked the app. I'd barely opened my eyes and laid a toe on my bedroom carpet when I saw that she was already over 4,000 steps ahead in the challenge that we are both now participating in. I was expecting a challenge because that's the whole point at the end of the day, but I hadn't realised just how quickly the gauntlet was going to be thrown down.

It seems that Jess is really up for the challenge, so I better make sure I put up a good fight.

There's still five minutes to go before I feel like it would be suitable for me to grab my coat and get out of here to start walking, but before I can watch those last few minutes tick away, I hear a male voice behind me.

46

'Hey, Lucy. How's it going?'

I swivel around in my chair to see Sean, one of my colleagues who isn't exactly a good friend but who I am always happy to chat to because he's nice, and he is also quite handsome, if a woman is partial to a scruffy mop of hair and some stubble, which I admit I am.

'Oh, hey. Yeah, I'm good. You?'

'Great. Busy morning?'

'The usual. But it's almost lunchtime, so I can't complain.'

'Yeah. That's what I was going to ask you about, actually. I was wondering if you fancied grabbing a bite to eat somewhere.'

'At lunch?'

'Yeah, I find that's usually a good time to eat.'

I almost forget to laugh at his joke because I'm still surprised by the fact that he has extended this invitation my way, but I recover, and the chuckle I give lets him know that he was quite witty then. But I still haven't answered his question.

'So, what do you say?' he asks me then. 'Lunch?'

'Erm…'

I look away from him and back at the clock to see that there is now only three minutes to go until I was planning on getting out of here and attempting to start chasing down Jess's step tally. But if I go for lunch with Sean then I won't be able to do that. Sure, I'll get a few steps in, but I won't get anywhere near as many as I would if I'm spending most of my break sitting in some café somewhere. I need to say no so that I can compete

47

with Jess. But I can't tell him that, or he'll most probably think I'm crazy. I mean, who turns down an invite for lunch so they can try and outwalk a virtual opponent they'll never meet?

'Don't worry about it, maybe another time,' Sean says after I have once again failed to answer him, and he turns to leave as if it's obvious what my decision was going to be. But I feel bad, so I call after him.

'Wait, I'm sorry,' I say. 'I was miles away. I've got a deadline coming up, and it's a little distracting. I didn't mean to be rude.'

'It's fine,' Sean says with a smile, and I'm relieved to see that he isn't too downhearted by my lack of enthusiasm to join him for lunch.

'I've just got something I need to do today. But another time though, yeah?' I say, and he gives me a nod before walking away.

It's only a couple of minutes later as I'm standing up to put my coat on that I realise it might not have just been a friendly invite. Maybe he was meaning it to be some kind of a first date between us. Does he like me? And if so, have I just totally ruined any potential romance between the pair of us?

I wonder if I should visit him at his desk before I leave the office and find out, but I chicken out of it and just head for the exit door, rushing down the stairs with my phone in my pocket recording the first few steps of my imminent sixty-minute break. When I get out into the sunshine, I squint, but I also silently curse myself for being stupid.

48

I've just rejected a guy I work with and have to see on a daily basis. Things could be awkward between us now, and awkwardness is the last thing anybody wants in the workplace. Maybe I should have just gone on the lunch date with him. It's not as if anything ever had to come of it. We could have just had a sandwich, a chat, and then gone back to our work. It would have been a normal way to spend a lunch hour. Instead, I'm going to be traipsing the streets trying to get my step count up just to beat this woman called Jess.

Maybe Kirsty was right.

Maybe this is why my love life is non-existent.

But once I've got walking properly and seen that I am closing the distance on the step counter between me and my opponent, I feel better about my decision. I'm a highly driven individual, so I shouldn't feel guilty about not wanting to fritter my break eating sandwiches, gossiping about colleagues and maybe even flirting a little. I have a challenge to win, and while it might not seem like an important challenge in the grand scheme of things, the very existence of it speaks to who I am at my core.

I like competing, and I like winning. There's no shame in that.

I bet Jess doesn't waste her time with lusting colleagues either. I bet she makes the most of every minute in her day and why shouldn't she? After all, we're only here once, and wasting time is no way to spend what time we have left.

My legs are carrying me quickly and easily around the park near my office, and I walk with a sense of freedom, loving the feeling of the sun on my face and the fresh air blowing in my hair. This is better than some cheap packaged sandwich and an overpriced coffee in a crowded café any day of the week. But it's as I'm preparing to make my third lap of the park when I spot Sean walking in the distance. But he isn't alone. He's with one of the girls from the finance team, and they are laughing away together as they go.

I guess he found somebody else to ask out for lunch. Good for him. I'm going to carry on with what I'm doing and ignore that slight pang of envy I can feel in the pit of my stomach. I'm not lonely. I'm doing what I want to do.

From that moment on, it's as if the whole park is suddenly flooded with couples walking by hand in hand or kissing and canoodling on the benches. All I seem to see are pairs of people laughing and joking while I stroll past them by myself. In the end, I decide to leave the park and finish the rest of my walk back on the busy streets. There seem to be less couples here, and Sean and that finance girl definitely aren't around.

By the time the sixty minutes are up, and I return to my office, I am feeling a little fed up, though I'm not quite sure why. That's why I decide to check my step counter to see how close I am to Jess now, presuming that I have closed the gap on her and made this into a real fight for the rest of the week. But to my dismay, I see that she has also been out walking too because she has not only managed to maintain her lead over me, but actually increase it by 500 steps.

Damn it. Maybe I should have gone for lunch with Sean after all.

No, that's not right. I want to win this contest. I'm just going to have to work harder to do it.

That's because, unlike many other people on this app, Jess is clearly a worthy opponent.

8

JESS

I love a good meeting. I particularly love it when I know that I am one of the items on the agenda, and that will be the case today as I wait for the director of the company to enter the room and take his seat at the head of this huge boardroom table to run through the sales figures for the past month.

In the meantime, I'm sitting patiently in one of the ten chairs around this imposing table and listening to the rest of my colleagues talking amongst themselves.

'Did you see the game last night?' one guy asks another.

'You'll never guess what Heather in HR sent me this morning,' one woman says to another.

And blah blah blah blah blah blah. I tune out of all the nonsense as it carries on, not at all interested in what anybody here is talking about because as far as I can tell, it has nothing to do with work, sales figures, and improving performance, and as long as that is the case, I have no interest in getting involved. One of them will be more than welcome to tap me on the shoulder and ask for my opinion if they want to know how to improve their performance or why I am about to get yet another bulging bonus in my bank account, but if not then I'll leave them be. But as they continue droning on amongst themselves, it's clear why I'm ahead of them all. They're so busy with the mundane aspects of life that they have lost sight of me zooming away over the horizon and leaving them languishing behind with their paltry figures and records.

There's Alan, the middle-aged guy twirling the wedding ring around his finger as he chats about football with Sam, the younger man who looks like he hasn't slept in days, and I doubt he has because he is the father to two young twins. There's Aly, the chatty, short-haired woman who is waffling on about some hen party she is attending this weekend in Amsterdam to Rochelle, the vivacious colleague who replies by saying she has a wedding to attend soon that she can't seem to find the right dress for.

There's a lot going on in this room, yet so little at the same time. I'm keenly aware that while I work with these people and have the same title as them, I am not like them. I'm not burdened by marriage and kids or umpteen amounts of social events that suck up all my spare time outside of the office. I keep things in my personal life simple and slick. No nonsense, not in the slightest.

In other words, it's all killer, no filler.

Do I feel like I'm missing out by not having a more well-rounded existence? No. If anything, it's they who are going to feel like they are missing out when they find out very shortly what the difference is in our respective pay this month.

It's a relief to see the director, Greg, walk in, looking smart as always in one of his trademark fitted suits. I respect a well-dressed man because it points to someone who cares about themselves, and if we can't care about ourselves, then who can? I don't need a husband to look out for me, or the love of a couple of kids to make me feel all warm and cosy about myself. Like Greg, I love myself, and there's no room for anyone else, which is why we're at the top of the food chain around here, and everyone else is feeding off our scraps.

'Okay, we'll keep this meeting short and sweet today,' Greg says as he unfastens one of the buttons on his suit jacket and exposes a little more of the expensive shirt and tie contained beneath. 'The sales figures are in, and it's been a good month. But it could have been better, and I'm sure you all know it. Sam, what happened to the Goldbridge account?'

I watch as Sam fumbles and mumbles his way through some answer about how the job he was in charge of securing ended up slipping through his fingers and going to a competitor. I'm also aware, as is everyone else around this table, that Greg will have already had Sam explain it to him privately in his office before this meeting started. But the fact the director is making his employee do it again here, in full view of the rest of the team, is evidence that in this environment, failure is not well received.

It takes poor Sam a while to give some kind of meaningful answer, but when he does, Greg simply regards it by looking back down at the file in front of him before moving on, showing that there is nothing more to say on the sorry matter.

Then the director gets to the good stuff.

'Jess,' he says, picking up the pace and volume of his speech as he moves from a negative subject to a positive one. 'It's been quite the month for you, wouldn't you say?'

'Yes, I suppose it has,' I reply with a smile as I feel the eyes of all my colleagues shifting onto me.

'That's actually an understatement. It's been a downright fantastic month for you. That's the truth. If only everyone could bring in the kind of clients that you do.'

'Thank you.'

'No, thank you. This month, your bonus will be twenty-five thousand pounds. And not a single penny of that is undeserved.'

I know I was expecting something good, but I didn't know it was going to be that good. 25k. Wow, now that is what I call a bonus.

'Erm, thank you. That's very generous.'

Greg rambles on about some more figures and bonuses after that, but I switch off because he's already told me what I need to hear. But I notice that a few of the other people around the table are still looking at me, and though they avert their gaze when I meet their eyes, it's obvious they are just as shocked by that figure as I was.

Does this kind of thing breed resentment in a team? I'm sure it does, but Greg knows what he's doing, and if anyone doesn't like it, they know where the door is. He's merely proving to them that I am the benchmark, and they are all chasing me.

The meeting concludes shortly after that, and everybody stands up to leave, some happy about their bonuses, some sad about the lack of one, but everyone still in awe of what I got. Nobody says anything to me as we filter out of the room, but that's not unusual. We'll chat about work if we need to, but other than that, we won't speak. My mind is already on next month's meeting now, and the aim is to get an even better bonus.

But as I get back to my desk and just before I prepare to pick up the phone and try to see if I can squeeze some business out of another prospective client, I check the app to see how I'm getting on in the steps challenge. When I do, I see that Lucy has been busy, although nowhere near as busy as she needs to be. Bless her, she is trying. But just like everyone I work with, she's going to have to do more than try if she wants to beat me.

Now, it's time to put my personal phone away and pick up my business one. But as I dial another client, I think about all the things I could spend my upcoming bonus on. I have many ideas, and I guess I'll go shopping this weekend to see what I can find on the high street. But that's not wasting time because it will come with the added benefit of getting my step count up.

See, I'm always thinking, and that, ladies and gentlemen, is why I'm always winning.

9

LUCY

I'm doing my duty, both as a good friend and a flatmate this evening. I've made myself scarce while Kirsty has her date over for a 'cosy night in', and I hope it's worth it for her. I'm sure she'll have fun, not that I'm going to spend too long thinking about what kind of fun she might be having. That's her business, not mine. But not being able to go home until at least ten o'clock this evening left me at a bit of a loose end.

I had considered all the options that I thought about earlier, like going shopping or catching a movie, or maybe even just going for dinner somewhere by myself. But in the end, none of them appealed enough for me to try them. There was only one thing that I felt like doing after giving it much consideration, and it's the most productive thing I could think of.

I'm walking in order to really make a difference in my challenge with Jess, and considering I have the whole evening to kill, I imagine I'm going to get a hell of a lot of steps in.

It's cold out tonight, but I have my coat and a pair of gloves on, and being on the move is doing enough to fend off the chilly air getting into my bones. Sure, I'd much rather be at home on the sofa now unwinding after a busy day in the office, but it's not as if I have to do this kind of thing all the time. Kirsty very rarely asks if she can have the flat to herself, and I know she would do the same if I requested it, not that I ever do. The only reason it would make sense for me to have the flat to myself would be for a guy to come around, and that isn't happening anytime soon.

I briefly think about Sean as I walk and what might have happened if I had gone to lunch with him. Could it have been the start of something between us? It's all ifs and buts, and if I'm honest, I'm not that attracted to him. It was flattering to get a little male interest, but being flattered isn't a good enough reason to start seeing someone romantically. There should be butterflies in the stomach and a deep yearning to be near that other person, and seeing as I don't have that with him, it doesn't seem worth entertaining anything else. Besides, it's not as if my life is empty without a man. I have plenty to keep me busy.

Like this challenge.

I'm enjoying it because it's become clear that Jess is very much up for the game too, and because of that, it's going to be a very hard-fought battle between us as this week goes on. Whoever wins will have earned it, and whoever loses will wonder if they could have pushed themselves just that little bit more to claim the victory.

There's nothing worse than that feeling of knowing you could have done more if you had really gone for it, but I always say that doubt is removed by action, and I'm certainly in action tonight. So far, I have walked all the way up the hill that overlooks this town before doing a lap of the old church building that sits up there before walking back down and onto the high street.

Now I'm passing all the busy bars and restaurants with the plan to turn left at the end of the street and do a circuit around the nicest part of town where the wealthier residents have their homes.

It's already been a big walk, and it's far from being over yet because I still have some time to kill until Kirsty will let me back in, but that's okay. This is fun. I'd rather be doing this, and I'll try not to spend too much time noticing the groups of women in the windows of the bars chatting and laughing away with a bottle of wine between them on the table. I'll also try to avoid all the couples I see going in and out of restaurants, big smiles on their faces as if they feel like they have everything they need in the world and nothing else matters.

To me, they all look comfortable, but that's not a place where legends get made. It's the uncomfortable moments that truly make us, and I have a feeling I'm going to be feeling very uncomfortable after all the walking I will have done this evening.

I've been listening to a podcast since I've been out here tonight. It's one about a successful entrepreneur who made his millions by the age of twenty-three and then wondered what to do next with his life. The podcast is his exploration of that as he travels the world, meets other high-achievers, and ponders what could be next for him. I've listened to a few episodes before during my commute or as I've been drifting off to sleep in bed at the end of the day, and it never fails to entertain me. It also never fails to make me feel like as successful as I am, there is so much more I could do. After all, I'm doing well at work, but this guy had made millions by an age where most people are just finishing university and figuring out what their first proper job might be.

By his standards, I'm a failure.

That thought causes me to quicken my pace because I don't like it.

It's a relief to eventually make it off the high street and away from the crowded venues, and now I'm in my favourite part of town. I love all the big houses here, and I make sure to have a good nosey at them as I pass them, peering through the gates that block the end of the driveways and seeing the looming mansions beyond. I've always told myself that I'll live here one day, buying myself one of these expensive properties because that will surely be the sign that I have made it in life. I'm not there yet, but I will be if I just keep pushing myself.

I notice one of the residents come out of his house as I pass it, and he gets into his rather expensive looking 4x4 before starting up the engine and giving the accelerator pedal a couple of revs before he gets going. As the gates to his property slide open and his vehicle moves out, he passes me, and I make eye contact with the man behind the wheel. But while I smile at him, he barely acknowledges my existence, and as he drives away, I feel myself feeling a little flat as I watch his tail lights disappear.

Was he rude? No, I don't think that was it.

He was probably just concentrating on what he was doing.

Or maybe he saw me walking and pitied me as he roared on by in his high-performance wheels.

I know it shouldn't bother me, but I hate the fact that someone could see me and think I wasn't up to their standards. It's almost as if I want to catch that guy up and explain why I am out here walking the streets at this time. I'd tell him it's because I'm competing hard against a stranger, and only one of us can win. Maybe that would garner me a little of his respect. He might be intrigued, and he might even be impressed, asking me if I do this kind of thing often and how fascinating it is that I go into competition against others on a regular basis. It shouldn't matter that he doesn't know anything about me, yet I feel like it does. I don't want him to think that I'm a loser because I'm a winner.

But there's only one way to prove that.

I have to beat Jess.

10

It's the last day of the step challenge, and I'm worried. I'm feeling that way because I'm currently losing, and I'm not sure if I'm going to be able to turn it around before the deadline. The app displays the ticking clock indicating how long is left for both Lucy and I to log our steps, and right now, there is only an hour to go.

I thought I would have had this victory wrapped up by now, assuming I would have been so far ahead that this final sixty minutes would have been nothing but a slow countdown to the inevitable. But now it seems this hour is going to be a desperate race for me to save face and avoid that one word that I despise above all others.

Defeat.

I've already been walking to work this morning in a bid to improve my chances, but as I see my office come into view, I realise that I'm still behind in the count. If I go to my desk and spend the morning sitting there dealing with emails and calls then my step count won't grow, and Lucy will win.

That is not an option, so I need a Plan B.

With that in mind, I decide to call Greg and ask my boss for a favour. I'm going to tell him that I'm going to be a little late to work this morning because I have an urgent errand to run. I won't go into specifics, and I doubt that he will make me. I'm his favourite employee, and I have certainly earned the right to ask a favour of him, so it should be okay. It's not as if I've ever made a habit of being late either.

'Hi, Greg. Good morning. How's it going?' I say into my phone as I turn away from my office and start walking in the opposite direction again, logging more vital steps as I go. 'I'm really sorry, but something has come up at home, and I think I'm going to be a little late in today. Is that okay? I'll make up the time, I promise.'

As I suspected, Greg doesn't have a problem with that, and after making me reassure him that it's not something terrible that has happened, he tells me to take my time and that he will see me when I get in.

I don't feel bad for lying to my boss, just like I don't feel bad for lying to anybody else. It's all just a means to an end. Results are the only thing that count in this world, and after what I've just done, I'm confident I'll get a better result in this step challenge.

I'm hoping that Lucy will not have just done the same thing that I have and got out of work for the next hour to keep walking, but I make sure to keep an eye on her step count to confirm it. Doing a challenge like this for the past week has given me a good indication of my opponent's routines and habits. I have an idea of what time she gets up in the morning, what time she goes for lunch, and how she spends her evenings, all by seeing when she walks and when she is stationary. Apart from one evening a few days ago when she seemed to be walking for hours, she has been fairly consistent with her movements. But it's that one random night that has put me at a disadvantage now because I've been playing catch-up ever since.

It's hard to really get up a brisk pace as I keep moving down the pavement, what with all the commuters rushing past me in the opposite direction, but I keep trying. But just before I can get away from this busy part of town and find a quieter street to really get motoring down, I hear somebody calling my name.

'Jess! Hey!'

I turn around and see that it's Sam from the office. He must have been amongst the sea of people that passed me, and now he has stopped me, presumably to ask me why I am walking in the wrong direction to work.

'Where are you going?' he wants to know.

'Erm…' I say, stalling while I try and come up with a good answer.

'Is the office on fire?' he asks jokingly.

'Ha. No, not quite.'

'Damn it. Maybe tomorrow then.'

He seems pleased with his sense of humour, and I don't bother telling him that if our office actually did burn down then he would have to find another job, and given his recent track record, he would probably be the one to find it the hardest.

'So, where are you going?'

He's not going to let me walk away without explaining myself, so I decide that it's time for another lie.

'I've just got something urgent to attend to. I called Greg, and he said it's fine. I'll be in soon. Okay?'

64

'Sure, no problem. I guess it pays to be the boss's favourite.'

Sam gives me a wink before telling me he will see me soon and walking away, and I watch him disappear amongst the crowd of commuters. I'm hoping he won't mention that he saw me out here to Greg, but there's not much I can do about it if he does. I can't be distracted by that now.

I just need to keep moving.

The next fifty minutes are spent with me walking all around the town centre, putting one foot in front of the other with the singular goal in mind. *Beat Lucy.* But as the end of the hour nears, one more check on the step count still has me at a disadvantage of just over 1,000 steps.

'Damn it,' I say as I stop walking, which won't help my cause either, but it's clear I need to try something else because what I'm doing isn't going to be enough.

There's only one thing I can do now.

I start running.

I must look ridiculous in my office attire, with heels on my feet and my handbag swinging away on my shoulder, but I don't care. This is the only chance I have left at increasing my step count enough to beat Lucy and win this challenge. Time has almost run out now, and I've never been so close to defeat.

But I'll do anything to avoid it.

Anything.

11

LUCY

I stumble on one of the steps in front of me before recovering and carrying on, going up and then down again as quickly as I can, all the while keeping my eye on the step counter on my phone. That's because it's so close between me and my opponent, and there's only ten seconds left.

It was only half an hour ago when I assumed I had victory already sewn up. I was ahead by a healthy margin, and I knew that Jess usually became a lot more stationary after 9am, where she presumably got to work and stopped walking so much. But then a strange thing had happened. Jess seemed to continue being on the move past 9am, and as the end of the challenge neared, her steps only increased in speed and volume.

I had no idea how she was doing it, but I had known I had to do something myself or she was going to steal victory away from me at the last minute. The only thing I could think to do was to come into the staircase of this emergency fire escape route in my office and start running up and down. It was either that or run around the main floor of the open-plan office, but that would have most likely seen me labelled as a madwoman, so I preferred this option. I might still be a slightly madwoman, but at least I'm being mad in private.

5,4,3...

Keep going, it's so close.

2...

Hustle, Lucy. Hustle!

1...

One more step. I need it!

Zero.

The beep from my phone is the notification to let me know that the challenge has just ended. No more steps will count towards our final tallies.

So, who has won?

I'm breathing heavily as I check the results, my heart racing thanks to all the physical exertion I've just done. I'm a little sweaty under my blouse and trousers, but there will be time to freshen up shortly. For now, it's about finding out if all that sweat was worth it.

And then I see that it was.

I've done it.

I've won!

'Yes!' I shout out loud, and my cry echoes around this empty stairwell.

I'm pleased with myself and the result, but it was a very close run thing. In the end, I beat my opponent by just 44 steps. That's nothing over the course of a week, and it's crazy that it came down to such a fine margin between the pair of us. But there can only be one winner, and that winner is me.

I feel like doing some kind of victory dance as I stand here on the third step of the staircase, but that would be immature. That's why I make do with just a small fist pump before putting my phone away and heading back to my desk, aware that I'm being paid to be here to work, not run around in the stairwell all morning.

After making a brief detour into the bathroom to make sure I wasn't looking too much of a dishevelled and sweaty mess, I take a seat in front of my computer again and let out a deep sigh. It's barely 10am, and I've already had my first win of the day. That bodes well for the rest of it to come, and I'm feeling so invigorated that I decide I'm going to make a few more business calls than I usually would today. But first, I must show some class and send my respect to my vanquished opponent.

The app allows its users to message one another if they wish, providing they don't send anything offensive or inappropriate, of course, so I will take advantage of that option and send a quick note to Jess to let her know how much I enjoyed that challenge and what a good competitor she proved herself to be.

'Hi! Wow, that was fun! And so close! I thought you had me beaten at the end there! Thanks for competing with me, and who knows, maybe we can take part in another challenge one day! But maybe not something so exhausting next time! Ha! All the best!'

I re-read the message to make sure that it comes across as fun and light-hearted before pressing send and delivering it to Jess's inbox. I expect she will reply to me at some point today, although maybe not. I guess it is a little weird to be messaging strangers over the internet, so she might not respond. Either way, I've done my bit by letting her know that I had a good time, and I didn't rub her face in my victory, so that makes me feel good about myself too.

The rest of the morning whizzes by in a blur of phone calls and emails, and it is lunchtime before I know it. I glance over towards Sean's desk and think about how I might return the invite for lunch to him to make up for turning him down last week. But when I do, I see him walking out of the office with a couple of other colleagues, already on their way to lunch and not stopping to ask me if I want to go with them. No bother, I brought a sandwich with me today, so I'll just sit and eat it in the kitchen. There might be someone else in there I can chat to anyway. But there isn't, so I end up eating alone, which doesn't bother me too much because at least I've got my phone for company.

I scroll through some fairly frightening news articles as I munch on my ham sandwich before deciding that I've read enough from these scare-mongering journalists for one day and go onto the app to see if there are any more challenges that I can take part in now that my latest one has finished.

I spend ten minutes looking, but nothing grabs my fancy, although I'll make sure to check back again soon because this app is constantly being updated with posts by other users. I've almost forgotten that I sent the message to Jess as I finish my food and prepare to leave the quiet kitchen, but when I do, I check my inbox to see if she has replied.

But there's no message from her. Oh well, maybe she hasn't seen it.

Then I see the tick beneath it, and it tells me she saw it and read it two hours ago.

I guess she isn't going to get back to me then.

I worry for a moment that I have offended her somehow by messaging her. Maybe it was too soon after the challenge ended. She was probably disappointed to have not only lost, but to have done so in such a close fashion. I know I would have been. Perhaps I should have waited a while before offering my commiserations and making jokes, or maybe I shouldn't have contacted her at all.

Oh well, it's done now, and I can't take it back. Anyway, I'm sure she's fine. She was probably just taking part in the challenge for fun. I doubt she was really taking it as seriously as I was. There are probably not many people out there who are as competitive as me. She's most likely busy getting on with the rest of the day, or maybe she has already started her next challenge. There's no better way to get over a disappointing defeat than to get right back to working on the next victory.

I make a check on Jess's profile to see if she has signed up for any more challenges because the app allows users to see what other people are currently competing in. But she hasn't signed up for anything else yet.

Never mind.

I wonder if she has stalked my profile page as much as I have stalked hers, but I doubt it because surely not everyone is as sad as I am. But that's enough snooping for one day, so I put my phone back in my pocket and leave the kitchen, carrying my empty lunchbox back to my desk whilst still feeling very hungry after my sandwich failed to do the job of filling me up.

Sean is not back at his desk yet, nor are any of the other colleagues he went out with, but that's none of my business as I return to my work, typing away on my keyboard and losing myself in my work again.

I keep my head down and stay busy for the rest of the day, but despite my earlier wave of extreme motivation and optimism after my victory in the step challenge, I don't end up making as many calls as I was planning to. If anything, I feel deflated and just want to go home and rest. I know what it is. It's that lull that always comes in between one competition ending and another one beginning. It won't last, and pretty soon, I'll have another big goal to focus on. But until then, I feel as if I'm existing in some kind of no man's land, drifting aimlessly through life.

I wonder if Jess feels the same way. Us competitive folk are very similar, I guess.

Who knows? Not me. Not unless she messages me back, anyway, which doesn't seem likely.

But as I leave my desk at the end of the day, I find myself checking the app in hopeful expectation one more time, just to see if she has replied.

She hasn't.

Oh well. Would I have replied to her? Possibly not.

Defeat is a bitch, after all.

12

I'm angry. Despondent. Frustrated.

And worst of all, *I'm a loser.*

I've been bathing in the shame of defeat all day, and it's not something I am familiar with, nor is it something I wish to get used to. This is not how things are supposed to be for me. I win. It's what I do. It's my whole identity. Or at least it used to be. But Lucy has changed that. She beat me, and most annoyingly, from what I can tell, she beat me fair and square.

No cheating. No lying. No deception. Just followed the rules and did what she had to do to be better than me. Now the challenge is over, and she has moved on with her life.

But I haven't moved on with mine.

I've read her message several times since she sent it to me this morning, not long after she had claimed victory by beating me by less than fifty steps. But no matter how many times I go through it word by word, it still stings. I don't want her sympathy, or respect, or good wishes. All those things are for the loser. I want sheer admiration or, better yet, nothing at all because that would suggest to me that my vanquished opponent is disconsolate and can't even bring themselves to congratulate me. I'll take that any day over what I have now, which is this woman, this Lucy, basking in the warm glow of her victory over me.

It's only a stupid challenge, I could say. Forget about it. It's not the end of the world. It's the taking part that counts. There will be other games and other opponents.

Yeah, right.

To me, that just sounds like the nonsense my school netball coach used to say after we had lost an inter-schools tournament, and he was trying to teach us that it wasn't all about the winning. But in reality, he was teaching us the wrong thing. He was talking absolute gibberish, and there's a reason he was coaching Under 9's netball at a local comprehensive school and not coaching highly-trained athletes at a World Cup. He didn't get it. He didn't understand the mindset that was needed to really achieve great things in competition.

But I got it. I've always got it. And that's why I've always won. *Until today.*

I want to reply to this message, and I want to say all the words that are rattling around in my head right now.

You bitch! I'm still better than you. Let's play another game. See if you can beat me then. I doubt it. You got lucky. It was a one-off. Lightning doesn't strike twice. You're inferior, and time will prove it. Let's go again. Pick the challenge. Whatever it is, I will wipe the floor with you this time.

Should I type all of that out and press send? I want to, I really do, but I don't, and I won't. How could I? It would look like the biggest load of nonsense a loser has ever spouted in their life. Lucy would probably laugh at me or worse, she wouldn't even reply at all, leaving me to stew forever and never get the chance to get that defeat back and put things back on an even keel. I can't have that. I need her to want to message me back and allow us to continue a dialogue until I have made things right again.

That's why I will go against all my instincts now and be nice to her. I'll write a message congratulating her, no matter how much it will make me feel sick to do so, because that is the best way of winning in the future.

Short-term pain for long-term gain.

I start typing, gritting my teeth as I write, just wanting to get this over with as quickly as possible.

'Hi, Lucy. Well done on the win. It really was close. We should do this again sometime. What do you say?'

I stare at the message, and apart from it making me feel nauseous with how weak it makes me look, I also feel like it isn't right. I could do more.

I have to do more.

Remembering that Lucy's profile said she was in the same town as me, I sense there is an opportunity here for me. Maybe we don't just have to compete virtually next time. What if we were to do it in person?

That would certainly be the best way for me to beat her because it would be so much more personal. But as well as that, I'm also intrigued about this woman enough to want to meet her and get to know her. After all, I haven't come across many worthy adversaries before, so it would be good to learn as much as I can about her. I want to know what makes her tick, her strengths and her weaknesses, information that I can use not to just beat her in whatever we do next but for future reference should I ever find myself in this unfamiliar position again with someone else.

With that in mind, I delete my original message and type out a new one, making sure this time to sound even more friendly and more fun because that will really disarm my rival and blindside her for what is to come.

'Hi, Lucy! Congratulations! You are right, that was a lot of fun! We both certainly worked hard to get those steps! It's a shame there had to be a loser, but never mind! If you don't mind me saying, I notice that we are both in the same town. How about we meet up for a drink? I'd love to meet a fellow player on this app, and it's obvious we are very like-minded with how competitive we are. So what do you say? And I promise there will be no step challenge this time!'

I'm happy enough with the message to send it and wait for Lucy's response. I'm praying that she takes me up on my offer of meeting up for a drink, but that remains to be seen. She could be a bitch and say no or just not reply, but I'm holding out hope that she won't be like that. I've made a very friendly gesture here, so there's no reason she won't be friendly back.

But I can't settle until I get her response, and I pace around my lounge with my phone in my hand, waiting for the notification that will let me know she has replied. Despite all my successes and all my accolades, all I care about at this moment is putting right the one loss on my record.

Come on, Lucy. Give me what I want. Give me a chance.

75

The beep from my phone lets me know I have a new message, and I stop pacing enough to check it. Sure enough, Lucy has replied, and when I read her response, a big smile spreads across my face.

'Hi! Thanks, a drink would be great! I'd love to! Do you have a time and place in mind?'

It's a small victory for me to get her to agree to meet me, and while it doesn't make up for the overall loss so far, it's a start back on the road to redemption for me.

'Awesome! How about Vinny's on Church Street? Say Friday or Saturday night? Whichever's best for you!'

I send my response to her and wait impatiently again. The fact I have just let her know that I am essentially free all weekend could make me look lame, but I don't have time to worry about things like that. The sooner I meet her, the better. But is she available at such short notice?

'Friday night works for me! 7:30?'

'Great! I'll see you then! You should be able to recognise me from my profile pic!'

'Cool! You too! See you Friday!'

With that, the date is set. I am meeting Lucy, the woman who beat me, and I'm very much looking forward to learning more about her. Is she just like me? Does she thrive on competition? Does she always win? If so, this is going to be a lot of fun as I try and beat her at something else.

Roll on Friday.

I cannot wait.

76

13

LUCY

One of the many joys of having a flatmate is that sometimes, I get home from work to find that my evening meal has already been made for me. Tonight is one such occasion because I've just walked through the door and been met with the wonderful sight of Kirsty putting the finishing touches on what appears to be fish tacos.

'Oh my God, I think I love you,' I say as I rush towards the kitchen counter where my flatmate stands and try to pick up one of the tasty tacos.

'Hey, hands off. Take a seat, and let's eat like civilised human beings,' Kirsty tells me, delaying my tastebuds the pleasure for a few more minutes.

But my friend is right. It's better if we sit, and we do just that, across the table from one another with the food in between us and a bottle of wine opened for good measure.

'How was work?' Kirsty asks me in between mouthfuls of salmon, and I tell her that it was fine in between my own mouthfuls.

'It was pretty quiet today,' I add. 'Again.'

'You still thinking of looking elsewhere?'

'Not sure. I do like it there. We'll see.'

Kirsty is referring to the few times I have mentioned that it might be worth me looking for a new job, just to push me out of my comfort zone and give me a fresh challenge. I'm doing well where I am, but I've been doing well there for a while, and things are in danger of getting predictable. I do sometimes entertain the idea of coming home and browsing a few job websites, but then I walk through the door and something else is always more interesting.

'But hey, in other news, I might have a new friend,' I say as I reach out to take another taco.

'Oh, yeah. Who's that then?'

'Jess, the woman I was competing against in that step challenge.'

Kirsty suddenly stops chewing and stares at me as if she is concerned by something she has just heard.

'What?' I ask her before taking another big bite.

'You're meeting one of the people from the app?'

'Yeah.'

'Do you think that's a good idea?'

'Why wouldn't it be?'

'It's a stranger on the internet. They could be crazy.'

'Says the woman who goes on dates with men she meets on the internet.'

'That's different.'

'How is it different?'

'I use proper dating sites. You're on some weird app.'

'It's not a weird app.'

'Any app where people compete against complete strangers is weird.'

I roll my eyes at my friend as she once again reminds me that she thinks one of the things I do as a hobby in my spare time is not the most normal thing in the world. Kirsty has always found it strange that I compete against people online, but I've never seen it like that. The internet is full of all sorts of things for all sorts of people with different vibes, and this is just my vibe.

'It's really no different to you meeting someone on a dating app. The only difference is I'm less likely to get an STD.'

'Hey! I have not had an STD!' Kirsty cries as a bit of salmon flies out of her mouth due to how much she is protesting. But I was only winding her up, and I apologise.

'I'm meeting Jess on Friday night,' I go on as I start to consider reaching for a third and final taco that really will push me to the limits of my intended calorie count for the day. 'And I don't care what you think. I'm looking forward to it.'

'Did you message her, or did she message you?'

'I messaged her first to say I enjoyed the challenge we had just finished. Then she replied and suggested we meet up, seeing as we're in the same town and everything.'

'So this meet up was her idea?'

'Yeah. And?'

'She's crazy.'

'How is she crazy?' I say, laughing at my friend's quick opinion on a woman she has never met before.

'Why would she want to meet you?'

80

'I don't know. To be friendly? To have a conversation with someone who has similar interests to her? That's what normal people do, isn't it? Find like-minded individuals to hang out with?'

'I don't know. I think you should be careful. Better yet, I think you shouldn't go on Friday.'

'Don't be ridiculous.'

'I don't want you getting murdered by some psycho you met on some weird app.'

'Funnily enough, I don't want that either. But I'm sure I'll be fine.'

I smile at my friend before opting out of the third taco, ultimately unwilling to put back on some of the weight I lost during all that excess walking I did in the step challenge.

'I can only imagine what kinds of things you two are going to talk about together,' Kirsty goes on as she finishes up her second taco. 'Bragging about what challenges you've done and who you've beaten recently.'

'We're not going to do that.'

'I bet you do. Oh God, it's going to be awful if this Jess becomes your friend and you introduce her to me. Then I'll have to put up with two of you instead of just one.'

'Don't worry, I'll keep her away from you,' I say with a chuckle before pushing my plate away from myself and leaning back in my chair.

I'm stuffed now, and I could easily just go and lie down on the sofa. But I should probably do the washing up, considering Kirsty did all the cooking, so

I'll get on with that as soon as my friend has finished eating. But my flatmate has gone for her third taco, clearly not as worried about her weight as I am mine, so I have a little more waiting before I can tidy up yet.

The rest of the meal is spent with me asking Kirsty about the guy she has been dating recently and when she plans on seeing him next. It sounds like it's going well between the pair of them, and I'm happy for my friend, although if things do get more serious between the two lovebirds, I might start to get worried that my flatmate might want her own place sooner rather than later. I'd miss us living together and not just because there would be nobody to make my fish tacos when I got home from work anymore. I'd miss her because I love seeing my friend every day and would have a void to fill if I started to see her a lot less.

But perhaps Jess could fill that void. If our meet-up on Friday night goes well then she could become my friend, and that would be an extra person for me to hang out with. Despite Kirsty's concerns about Jess being some kind of internet weirdo, I'm optimistic about that not being the case. But I won't know that until I arrive at the bar and see her.

Fingers crossed, I don't take one look at her and want to run for the door.

After finishing up the meal and clearing away, I join my flatmate on the sofa where we chat some more while watching some cookery programme set in Naples that really makes me want to go there for both the food and the scenery. But I also find myself spending a part of the evening looking at Jess's bio on the app to see if I

82

glean any more information about her before we meet in person. In other words, I'm scouring for any clues that might confirm Kirsty is right and Jess is someone to be avoided. But there is nothing that makes me worry. Her photo, description and general stats on this site all seem normal, although there is one thing that stands out to me.

It's her win percentage on this app, which is the calculation that shows how often she wins the challenges she takes part in with other users.

It's at an astonishing 99%.

That means she has hardly ever lost. But I beat her, and for that, I'm very much in the minority.

But I doubt the fact that I'm possibly the only person on this app to ever conquer her is the motivating factor behind her wanting to see me. It really will just be because we're local to each other, and it makes sense for us to see if we could be friends. I'm sure Jess wouldn't have been interested enough in seeing me if we were at opposite ends of the country.

That's enough looking at her profile page to try and learn things.

Soon enough, I'll be able to find out everything I need to know about her in person.

14

JESS

I'm early, I'm smartly dressed, and I'm nervous as I enter the busy bar and approach the woman behind the small stand, upon which sits an open book that presumably lists all the table reservations for this venue this evening.

'Hi, I have a table booked under Jess for two at seven-thirty.'

'Ahh, yes, the table is ready if you'd like to follow me.'

I do just that, tailing the friendly hostess as she shows me to the table where I will shortly be sitting with Lucy.

I don't order a drink to keep me occupied while I look out for her to arrive, instead opting to wait until she is here before making any decisions that will telegraph information about myself. I don't know whether or not Lucy drinks alcohol, so I don't want to give her that answer about me without making her work just as hard for it.

First impressions are everything, in all walks of life, but just as much so in a situation where two highly competitive individuals are coming together for the first time. We will be sizing each other up, non-verbally at first, before we even start asking questions of each other to prise more information out that way. We'll judge each other on appearances, demeanour, and whether or not either one of us is most comfortable with a glass of water in front of them or a cocktail.

I've done my best to make this whole situation appear as though it is a friendly coming together of two people who potentially could be friends, but really, it's all about me getting a good read on this other woman and figuring out what it is that I can beat her at in the future to restore my damaged pride.

The benefit of having seen Lucy's profile pic allows me to spot her the moment she enters the bar, and I make sure to sit a little higher in my seat and roll my shoulders back as she walks in, sees me and approaches the table.

Right now, her brain will be processing all sorts of information, but all I can do is make myself look as confident, strong, yet still as friendly as I can.

'Hi. Jess?' she says a little tentatively as she reaches my table, and I allow one second of silence between us to make her doubt herself before I smile and get up from my seat.

'Hey, Lucy! You made it! Great to meet you!' I say as I open out my arms to let her know that we are to come together for a hug.

I could have opted for a handshake, but that would have seemed too formal and might have kept Lucy on edge in the earliest beginnings of our interaction, so I'm disarming her by being uber-friendly and welcoming.

She hugs me, lightly and quickly, before we take our seats opposite one another.

'I thought I'd wait until you got here before I ordered any drinks,' I say as I look over at the bar behind Lucy.

'That's fine. Wow, it's busy in here tonight, isn't it? I've not been here for a while.'

'Me neither. I'm glad I reserved a table.'

'Oh, yeah. Thanks for that.'

I smile to accept Lucy's thanks, and it was what I was seeking when I reminded her that I made the reservation because getting her to thank me is a subtle way of making it seem like I am in charge here and am calling the shots.

'So, what do you want to drink?' I ask, staying in control early.

'Erm, I'm not sure. What are you thinking?'

She isn't bold enough to make a decision without first gauging what I am intending to do.

Interesting.

'How about a glass of wine?'

'That sounds good!'

I smile at Lucy, who does seem very eager, before attracting the attention of one of the wait staff and placing our order with them. Again, I'm taking charge of proceedings, and the fact that Lucy is happy to let me do so only makes me more annoyed that I lost to her at something in the first place. She seems passive so far.

'So, Lucy. What do you do for work?'

'I'm in recruitment. I work for various clients who entrust me with finding the right candidate for them.'

I'm even more intrigued now because it seems that Lucy's job is not too dissimilar to my own. It might be a different industry, but it requires the same skills like selling and managing clients, so it sounds like we have even more in common than just competing on the same app.

'Oh, wow. That's cool,' I say, remembering to play nice and pretend like I really want to be her friend. 'I hear that can be a tough industry to work in.'

'Yeah, it can be. But I like it, and I've been doing it for years now.'

'Oh, really?'

It's funny how quickly a picture can begin to form about another person. All I knew about Lucy five minutes ago was what she looked like and that she was competitive, but now I know her profession, the fact she has been in the same line of work for a while, and also that she drinks alcohol because she was happy to agree with my suggestion of wine. It's all information that I can store away and potentially use at a later date to my own advantage.

'Do you get a salary, or is it commission based?' I ask, getting another question in before she can fire one at me and start learning my life story. 'I hear different recruitment companies do things differently.'

'I get a base salary, but there are bonuses too,' Lucy admits, and the way the edges of her lips slightly curl up just after she has answered me gives me a hint that she likes the fact there are bonuses in her company, and she is no stranger to them.

'What about you?' Lucy says, finally taking charge. 'What do you do for work?'

I could lie here and make up a story to keep her in the dark because she doesn't need to know the truth that I'm a super saleswoman who lives for beating my business rivals and securing lucrative bonuses. That's because anything I do tell her in honesty could be used to her advantage in whatever realm we compete in next. But I want this to be a fair fight, for now, anyway, so I'll play nice and tell the truth.

I fill Lucy in about what I do but make sure not to brag about how good I am at it or how wealthy it is making me, before a waiter serves us our drinks.

'Cheers,' I say as I pick up my glass and hold it out towards Lucy. 'Thanks for coming out. It could have been weird, but I think we're going to have fun.'

'Me too,' Lucy replies with a warm smile. 'Cheers.'

With that, we clink glasses and take a sip, and now the evening has really begun.

We spend the next hour talking about our experiences on the app that brought us together, telling tales about the various challenges we have taken part in, what we think the app could do better for its users, as well as the fact that we checked out each other's bio to see how the other one had been faring on the site. Lucy pleases me by letting me know that she noticed my 99% win rate, before irritating me by asking if she is the only person who has beat me so far.

I laugh that suggestion off and say there were one or two others, which is a lie, before I finish my wine while imagining smashing this glass over her head for saying that she beat me.

We also discuss what drove us to download the app onto our phones in the first place. That's where I get confirmation that Lucy is a very competitive person just like me because she admits as much, telling me that she has always thrived on challenging herself to do better than other people, even if she's not exactly sure why she's wired that way. I tell her that I am the same, and our bond only gets stronger, reinforced by Lucy's desire a moment later to make our next drink not just a glass of wine each, but a full bottle to share.

She's having fun. She's at ease.

In other words, she's right where I want her.

Now it's time for me to get that one defeat back, and I want it now. It doesn't have to be anything big, and I can make it sound like it's just a fun game, but I need it because every second she holds a 1-0 record over me is offensive.

'Seeing as we like a little competition, how about we play a friendly game?' I say as I display a cheeky smile.

'What are you thinking?' Lucy wants to know, her own expression showing that she is up for some fun if I am.

'Let's see who can get the most phone numbers by the end of the night. We've got three hours until this place closes and the crowds will recycle. There's plenty of guys in here, and there'll be plenty more coming in to replace them when they leave. So what do you say? You want to play?'

Lucy initially seems a little unsure, and I worry that she isn't going to give me that chance to get a win back so soon, but then she nods her head as she looks around at all the other tables in here, many of which have guys sitting at them having a good time.

'Let's do it,' she says with a confident smirk. 'Game on.'

15

LUCY

'Hi, excuse me. Sorry to interrupt, but I was wondering. Could I get your number?'

I stare at the man I have just spoken to while silently praying that he won't just laugh in my face and go back to his conversation with his friends. He looks back at me and doesn't say anything for a moment, making me doubt myself even more, and I'm wishing I hadn't bothered playing this game that Jess has come up with.

But then he smiles.

'Sure,' he says. 'Do you want me to put it in your phone?'

'Oh, yeah. Right!' I say, almost forgetting that I actually need to make it look like I'm going to save the number he's about to give me. I'm only doing this to try and win the challenge Jess has set, not because I'm on the prowl for a new boyfriend, but this guy doesn't need to know that.

He tells me his number as I type it into my device, and then I thank him and wish him a good night.

'Hey, where are you going?' one of his friends asks me. 'You don't even know his name yet!'

I pause, aware that it probably does look a little weird of me to come over here, get a number and then scurry away quickly without at least trying to learn a little bit more about the man I've just procured the digits from.

'Sorry,' I say with a nervous laugh. 'I don't usually do this kind of thing.'

'I don't think any woman does,' the object of my attention replies. 'I can't remember the last time a woman came up to me and asked for my number.'

'Yeah, it's pretty unusual,' his friend agrees.

I already know it's unusual because it's generally the man who approaches the woman, and I've certainly never made a habit of going up to strangers. That explains why I'm feeling so jittery now. I'm very much out of my comfort zone here. But I only need to glance to my left, where I see Jess talking to a guy over there, to remind myself why I am doing this.

This is a game, and I am trying to beat her.

'So, what's your name?' I ask the guy who just gave me his number.

'Ryan,' he tells me. 'And you are?'

'Lucy,' I say before putting out my hand to shake his.

'Nice to meet you, Lucy. Would you like a drink?'

'Oh, erm, thank you, but I should really be getting back to my friend.'

'She can join us if she likes?'

'Erm, maybe.'

I'm realising now that the hard part of this game isn't getting the phone number. It's getting away afterwards. Ryan is clearly thrilled that I approached him, and perhaps unsurprisingly, he wants to seize on the

92

opportunity rather than let me walk away and potentially change my mind about calling him in the future.

But I need to move on because my competitive side is reminding me that one phone number won't be enough to win the challenge. I can already see Jess talking to her second guy on the other side of this crowded bar now, and presumably, that means she'll be winning 2-1 now.

'I better go,' I say.

'Okay, cool. I'll hopefully speak to you soon,' Ryan calls after me as I rush away, squeezing myself in between a large group of women who are standing by the bar, before looking around for someone else to go and talk to.

This is certainly not what I was expecting to be doing when I came out to meet Jess this evening. I imagined we would just chat and get to know each other, not start playing another game. But this new challenge was Jess's idea, and I guess she's even more competitive than I thought. But I don't mind. I like it, and this is certainly more exciting than just chatting about work or TV programmes. I can do that with Kirsty, but Jess is different.

She is like me.

I see a guy in a blue shirt leaning against the edge of the bar a few feet away, and he seems to be on his own as he orders a drink, so I swoop in and ask for his phone number before I can talk myself out of it.

He's just as surprised as Ryan was to be approached by me but also just as eager to give me his phone number before I can change my mind. He also offers me a drink, and I'm thrilled that the men in here are being such gentlemen, even if I'm not actually interested in them, before I politely decline and walk away.

Now I'm heading back to my table where I plan to take a little break from this game and see how my rival has been getting on. Jess was right, we can't just go around to every guy in here because that would look suspect. This is a game to be played over the course of the evening as some guys leave and new guys enter.

I can see Jess has already made it back to our table, and she is looking at her phone, making me wonder just how many phone numbers she has already managed to get in there. Am I already behind, or am I winning? I won't know until I ask her, but just before I get back to the table, I spot a couple of guys walking towards me, and I seize my chance to potentially take the lead in this challenge.

'Can I have your number?' I call out before the two men can pass.

They both stop and look at each other with confused expressions before looking back to me.

'Sorry, which one of us were you talking to?' the first guy asks me, and I realise that I didn't exactly make that clear when I fired my question at them. But eager to win this challenge, I decide to go for broke.

'Both of you,' I reply.

'You want both of our numbers?'

'Yeah.'

'Really?'

'Is that okay?'

94

The two friends share another confused glance before shrugging and saying that would be okay, even though it's a little weird.

I take down both of their numbers and thank them, and they walk away laughing between themselves before I get back to my table.

'Hey!' I say as I retake my seat opposite Jess. 'Oh my God, that was so stressful, wasn't it?'

'Yeah,' Jess replies, looking up from her phone. 'So, how many numbers did you get?'

'I got four,' I tell her, hardly believing it myself. But Jess seems even more shocked.

'Four! In just five minutes?'

'Yeah. How many did you get?'

'Two.'

'Oh, well done!'

'I notice then that we don't have any wine in front of us, so I suggest another drink. But Jess hasn't heard me, instead just getting up from her seat again.

'Where are you going?' I ask her.

'To get more numbers. We're still playing, aren't we?'

'Erm, yeah. I suppose. I just thought we were having breaks too.'

'Never mind that. Let's change the rules. How about first to ten.'

'Ten numbers?'

'Yeah, that okay?'

'I don't know. That's a lot.'

'Don't think you can do it?'

'I didn't say that. I just thought it would be nice to have another drink and a chat.'

'There'll be time for that after. First one to get ten numbers comes back to the table. Loser buys the rest of the drinks all night. Deal?'

I can see Jess is really keen to carry on with this game, so I agree to it, and she rushes away across the bar in the direction of the nearest man before I've had a chance to say anything more.

I guess we are playing again, so I get back to my feet and look around for someone else to talk to. But before I go asking for any more numbers, I can't help but feel like Jess might be taking this all a little too seriously. I mean, I know we both like to compete, but she might be taking that to another level to me.

Is that a bad thing though? Perhaps I need someone like this in my life. Maybe it's what has been missing all along. Someone who understands, like I do, that life is not supposed to be easy. It's supposed to be about constantly striving for more.

More sales. More money. More phone numbers.
More wins.

This might only be the first night I have met her, but I already get the sense that this won't be the last time I see Jess. I have a feeling we're going to have a lot of fun together.

But which one of us has the most fun remains to be seen.

16

I've got eight numbers now, but I can't stop until I have two more and beat Lucy back to the table. She was ahead of me earlier when I checked, and she could still be ahead of me now, for all I know. I can't see her in this busy bar because it's getting to that peak time on a Friday when it feels like half the town has come out to have a drink and unwind after a long week. But just because I can't see my rival, it doesn't mean I don't know she isn't out there hustling to try and beat me.

So I have to hustle harder.

'Hey! Can I get your number?'

I've surprised the man in the suit standing beside me with my loud question, and he stops sipping his whiskey to look me up and down. But I don't have all day for him to make a decision. Speed is everything here.

'What is it?' I ask him again as I hold my phone out, ready to type on it.

'I'm sorry. What's going on?'

'I just want to get your number.'

'Why?'

'Why do you think?'

I give him a suggestive smile there that will hopefully help seal the deal. But he only looks flustered by that, and not in a good way.

'I can't,' he tells me.

'Of course you can. What is it?'

'No, I mean, I really can't.'

'Why?'

'I'm married.'

Damn it. A married guy will never give me his number. I should have taken a second to check his left hand for any sign of a ring instead of rushing in my haste to try and beat Lucy. Now I have just wasted several precious seconds. *Unless...*

'Don't worry, I won't tell your wife if you don't,' I say before winking, hoping that uncaring attitude might be enough to get him to forgo his wife's feelings and give me his number anyway.

But it doesn't work, and the man just looks disgusted by what I have said, so I scurry away before he can admonish me for my actions.

What I just said might have been slightly heartless, but it's not as if I'm ever going to call any of these men who give me their numbers tonight. I couldn't care less about any of them. I just have to beat Lucy. If anything, meeting her has only served to make me feel even worse about the fact that she beat me because now I've seen how happy, confident and assured of herself she is. She basically looks and feels like how I used to before I lost to her. That defeat has stolen something from me, and it's a part of myself that I have to get back. I want her to be brought back down to Earth instead of swaggering around this place thinking she is somehow better at things than me.

I spot another guy and rush over to him, catching him before he can finish putting his coat on to leave.

'Hey! I'm really sorry, but I just have to do this. Please can I have your number?'

The man seems interested in what I have just said to him, or at least he does right up until the moment his partner returns to the table from the toilets with her coat on, also ready to leave.

'Who's this?' she asks him, referring to me, but I turn and hurry away before he answers, leaving him to come up with some story that won't make his wife or girlfriend jealous or mad at him.

I'm really on a bad run of luck here. It shouldn't be this hard for a woman like me to get a phone number from a guy, but I'm starting to wish I'd picked a different challenge now. I did think about just ordering a load of shots of tequila and seeing which one of us could drink the most, but I decided against that because I really could do without the hangover tomorrow. I also considered an arm wrestle but thought that might be a weird thing for two women to do. In the end, I decided on this challenge but only because I figured it was one I could win.

I thought that because, in my admittedly biased opinion, I believe I'm more attractive than Lucy. It's not that she isn't pretty, it's just that I think I'm prettier. Because of that, I figured I would have an easier time getting phone numbers from men than she would. But perhaps I underestimated just how eager all men are when approached by a woman, or maybe I just

99

underestimated how determined a competitor Lucy really is. If so, I have made a mistake, and I should have known better because she already demonstrated to me during the step challenge that she could be disciplined and relentless.

But I can be those things too, and I'm certainly going to have to be if I have any chance of winning.

Still lacking the two numbers I need to get to ten and return to our table, I spot two guys sitting in the back corner of this bar, and I make a beeline towards them, wondering if I could somehow get both their digits at the same time so that I don't have to go looking for anyone else after this.

'Hi, guys, you don't mind if I join you, do you?' I say before sliding into the booth and taking a seat at the table with them without waiting for their response.

'Erm, sure. No problem,' the first guy replies before taking a nervous sip of his beer while his friend smiles at me awkwardly.

'I'm going to be honest with you both. I've just been dumped by my boyfriend, and I'm feeling pretty low. What I need is a reminder that I'm not ugly or going to be on my own forever, and I'm trying to do that by coming over and seeing if you might give me your phone numbers?'

'Wait a minute. Didn't you just speak to us?' the first guy says before the other guy interjects.

'No, that was someone else. Her friend, maybe.'

'What are you talking about?' I ask, a little confused.

'Some other woman just asked for our phone numbers.'

'Did you give her them?'

'Yeah, we did.'

Damn it.

'Oh, okay. But can you give me your numbers too?'

'Not if you're just doing it to play some weird game.'

'It's not a weird game.'

'Forget it. Go find someone else's time to waste.'

'Guys, it's not like that. Seriously.'

'Have a good night,' the first guy says before starting up another conversation with his friend, leaving me sitting there beside them feeling like an idiot.

I can see that I'm never going to be able to convince them to give me their numbers now, so I stand up and leave the booth, figuring I'll just have to find someone else to try now. But then I have an idea. Just because I didn't get them to give me their numbers, it doesn't mean that I can't pretend I did.

Typing in my phone, I put in two fake numbers, ones that aren't real, but Lucy won't know that. I could show them to her, and she'll just think they were given to me by some of the guys in here. And now that I've done that, I have ten.

That's all I need to win.

Rushing back across the bar, I am eager to get seated at the table so I can be sitting there before Lucy returns, and it will be a pleasure to see the look on her face when she finds out that she has lost. But then I freeze in the middle of the busy bar, staring straight ahead at the sight across from me.

I can see Lucy, and she is already sitting at our table with her phone in her hand and a smile on her face.

She waves when she sees me before gesturing for me to come over and join her.

Unfortunately, I know why that is.

It's because she has just won again.

17

LUCY

'Come on, one more drink! Let's try in here!'

I open the door to the only pub that looks like it is still open in town, and Jess follows me in, still seeming reluctant to carry on our night because it is late now, but I have managed to convince her to delay going home and going to bed a little longer. I've done that because I'm having a great time, and I don't want it to end yet. This has been one of the best Friday nights I've had in ages, and I'm thrilled that I seem to have made a new friend.

'Two gin and tonics, please, landlord!' I say to the old man on the other side of the bar, who wearily trudges over to the gin bottles and starts preparing our drinks. He was probably hoping to close up soon, but now we're here, he has one last job to do.

'Cheers!' I say to Jess once we receive our drinks. 'Here's to doing this again soon!'

I take a gulp of my fizzy drink before grimacing because it's a little stronger than I had been expecting. My head is going to be really sore tomorrow, but I'll deal with that when it comes.

'So, are you going to call any of the guys?' I ask Jess a moment later after a brief lull in the conversation that has me worried my companion might be regretting coming in here with me instead of just ordering the taxi she had been talking about ever since we left the last place.

'What? No, of course not!'

'Why not?'

'It was just a game.'

'I know, but it doesn't mean you can't have some fun. You're single, right?'

'Yeah.'

'And there must have been at least one guy you spoke to who you found attractive.'

'I suppose.'

'Then give him a call!'

Jess doesn't seem convinced, so, in my tipsy state, I try to grab her phone.

'Look, I'll do it for you,' I say, trying to use her phone to call one of the numbers she got. But she takes it off me and shakes her head, clearly not finding it as amusing as I am.

'Why don't you call one of the numbers you got tonight?' she asks once she has been able to get her device away from me.

'Meh, I don't need the hassle of a man right now.'

'Really? Why's that?'

'I don't know. I just want to focus on my career.'

'I thought you were doing well in recruitment.'

'Yeah, I am. But I'm worried I'm in my comfort zone. Maybe it's time to do something else.'

'Like work for a different recruiter?'

'Maybe. Or maybe a complete career change. A new industry. New challenges. That would be cool.'

I'm aware that I've reached that point of drunkenness where I start getting all philosophical and talking about my desire to change my life. It's something that I've heard many other people do before as the alcohol in their system is all they need to finally wake up and make a change before the inevitability of death comes for them at some point down the line.

'I feel like I could do more,' I say, chattering on without giving Jess a chance to speak. 'Earn more. Be more. Live more.'

'I don't know. Just because you're good at one place, it doesn't necessarily mean you'll be good in another.'

I'm surprised that my companion isn't a little more supportive of my desire to make a change, but I suppose she is just being sensible. I guess all the wine and gin hasn't quite gone to her head as much as it has gone to mine.

I fear then that I might be annoying her, so I decide to stop waffling on about myself and try and make this conversation a little more interesting for her.

'What about you?' I ask as I watch the old barman putting several dirty glasses into a dishwasher. 'Do you think you'll keep doing what you're doing? Are you happy?'

'I'm the best at what I do,' Jess replies with a small hint of arrogance, but I put it down to the drink talking rather than a personality trait. 'Why would I stop?'

'I don't know. For the challenge? You obviously like to compete against others, and your 99% win rate on the app tells me you're damn good at it too. Although perhaps it should be 98% now after I beat you with the phone number game.'

I meant what I just said as a joke, but I fear I've pushed it too far because I see a flash of annoyance on Jess's face before she covers it up with a large glug of her drink.

'I'm only joking. It was just a game.'

'It's fine,' she tells me, but I'm not sure that it is.

Oh, no. Have I screwed this up? Is she not going to want to see me again? I really hope not because I want to see her again. She's by far the most interesting person I know.

'Let's change the subject,' I say. 'Or better yet, let's get another drink.'

I try and get the attention of the barman, but Jess tells me she has really had enough this time and wants to get going. She proves it by using her phone to book herself a taxi before I have a chance to talk her out of it again.

'Oh, okay. I suppose it is late,' I say, trying to cover up how disappointed I am by pretending like I wouldn't happily have stayed out here all night with her if I could. I guess I'll just go home and have a nightcap by myself, unless Kirsty is still awake, which I hope is the case because then I'll be able to tell my old friend all about my new friend.

At least, I still think Jess is my new friend. But as she stands up and puts her coat on quickly, I feel like I need to double-check she isn't leaving me in a bad mood.

'Do you want to do this again?' I ask, not wanting to sound needy but not sure how else to ask that question without just wording it like that.

'Yes, definitely,' Jess replies, to my relief. 'But let's do something different next time.'

'What do you have in mind?'

'I'll think of something.'

'Oh, okay. Well, just give me a text when you do!'

I grab my coat and follow Jess out of the pub, thanking the barman as I go, but he just grumpily watches me leave, probably glad he can finally lock the door and go to his bed now before waking up to do it all over again.

It's cold outside the pub as I stand with Jess and wait for her taxi to arrive. I've not ordered one because it's only a short walk home from here for me, and I could use the five minutes of fresh air to sober me up a little before I get in. But I'll wait here anyway to make sure Jess gets away okay.

'How about a marathon?' Jess suddenly says as we stand shivering on the street.

'What?'

'A marathon.'

'What do you mean?'

'You mentioned wanting to do something again.'

107

'Well, yeah, but I meant like a drink or a meal.'

'Why? That's what everyone else would do. I thought you wanted a challenge?'

'Erm…'

'If you don't think you can do it then we can find something else.'

'No, that's not it.'

'Great! There's a marathon coming up next month.'

'Next month? That's a bit short notice.'

'Afraid of a little challenge?'

'No, I didn't say that.'

'Then we'll do it. It's not hard. All you have to do is put one foot in front of the other.'

'For twenty six miles!'

'Meh, the distance is irrelevant.'

I'm surprised by how casual Jess seems to be describing a marathon, which leads me to think she must have ran one before. But when I ask her if she has, she shakes her head.

'No. But it's something I've always wanted to do. So, are you in with me?'

I think about it, but I'm not sure how I can say no now. My competitive instincts won't let me.

'Screw it. Yeah, I'm in!' I say with a laugh, and Jess smiles, just as her taxi arrives and parks up in front of us.

'So, are we going to train together or what?' I ask Jess before she can disappear into the back of the vehicle.

'Yeah, I'll text you,' she says before closing the door, and I give her a wave as she drives away.

Watching the taxi's headlights moving away down the street, I can't help but feel that was a little weird. She wants to run a marathon with me? We've only just met. She really is different to anyone else I know.

But now I've said yes, I can't go back on that. I've committed to it. I suppose it's not a bad thing because I've always wanted to run a marathon too.

I guess I better get training.

18

JESS

I don't say a word to the taxi driver as he drives me home, choosing instead to sit in silence and stare out of the window at the dark houses we are passing by. But while I might seem calm and passive on the outside, my insides are a churning mess.

That bitch beat me again. That's twice now that we have gone head to head and twice that she has come out on top. There's no way that I can let her beat me a third time.

That would be unthinkable.

I'm seething as I recall the 98% joke Lucy made to me back at the pub, referring to my winning percentage on the app and how it should be adjusted after I had lost to her again. Who the hell does she think she is, mocking me like that? I'm aware that she probably didn't mean anything nasty with it and was just trying to have a laugh because she was very eager to be my friend, but still, I can't let her get away with a comment like that.

I can't let her go on in life thinking that she can beat me in whatever game we play.

That's why I suggested the marathon. I needed something for us to do, but I wanted a little time to prepare for this next challenge. The phone number game in the bar was a spontaneous idea, and in hindsight, it was a foolish one because I was at as much of a disadvantage as Lucy was. Neither of us had any time to get ready for that, we just had to do it, so the odds really were 50/50. Even though I would always back myself at those odds, unfortunately the outcome didn't go in my favour. But now I have suggested a challenge with a longer timescale to it, I can make sure that I get an advantage. I'll out-train her so much that by the day of the marathon, the odds will be overwhelmingly in my favour.

And I'm going to get started tonight.

'Just here,' I say to the taxi driver as I see my property come into view, and I waste no time in getting out of the vehicle and rushing up to the front door with my key in my hand. I stumble a little as I go, a consequence of all the drinks I have put into my system this evening, but I'm not going to let a little inebriation stop me from what I am planning on doing.

Once inside, I go into my bedroom and pull open the wardrobe doors, rummaging around in there for my gym clothes and my trainers. I put them on as soon as I find them and then head back to the front door, bracing myself for the cold air as I open it and step back outside again. It might seem like madness to go for a run by myself in the middle of the night and especially after a night out in which I had more than my fair share of wine and gin, but I don't care. There will be no way I can get to sleep anyway, not with all the thoughts of Lucy beating me whirling around in my head. That's why I will come out here and start running, and I'm not going to stop until I reach the point of exhaustion.

As I set off running down the quiet street, I'm aware that I am fully in training now. I will not stop preparing for the marathon until it is here because that will be the day I put this right. From now until then, every bit of food I put into my mouth will be selected carefully and only consumed if it will help me in my goal of getting in shape for the marathon. So will every bit of exercise I undertake, and every early night I have. Everything in my life now revolves around finishing that marathon ahead of Lucy.

But I don't just want to beat her and show her that I can be a better long-distance runner than her. I want to demolish her by finishing so far ahead of her that she is embarrassed to have even participated in the marathon at all. I want to be standing at that finish line an hour before she gets there, and I want her to see me as she finally comes around the final bend, exhausted and out of breath. I want her to see that I did it better than her, and then I want her to apologise for that 98% remark. She might think that I'm joking, but I'll be deadly serious. Then, when she has apologised and only then, will I tell her the truth. I'll tell her that I never had any intention of being her friend and that I only wanted to meet her because she beat me at something, and I couldn't rest until I had beaten her at something too. I'm sure she will be shocked by that, and she might even think I'm pathetic, but I won't care. I'll just rub my victory in her face, and then I'll be gone, able to get on with my life again without the thought of her holding superiority over me.

The sound of my trainers hitting the cold concrete is loud at this time of night with no other soul around. All the lights in these houses are off, and all the residents are tucked up in their beds, getting their rest before their own challenges ahead. If any of them were to wake up and look outside now, peering past their curtains at the lone woman jogging down their street, then I am sure they would think I was stupid. But to me, they are the stupid ones. They are wasting time while I am maximising it. They are stagnating while I am getting stronger. And I know that right now, Lucy will be no different to all these people in their beds.

There's no way that she will be out running now. She'll be back home, either having another drink or getting ready to get under her duvet, possibly still feeling smug about getting ten guys' phone numbers faster than I could get them. In other words, she'll still be basking in victory while I am already out here plotting her next defeat. There's no way she'll beat me at this. She's competitive, but I'm on a whole different level, and she's going to find that out soon enough.

But I must be careful. There's a good reason one of the most oft-quoted expressions ever is "keep your friends close but your enemies closer." It's because it's very true. It would do me no good to not see her too much before the day of the marathon because then I won't know how well her preparation is going. I need to measure and monitor her progress, while at the same time concealing mine and lulling her into a false sense of security. That's why I'll make sure to catch up with her regularly. We can go for a few runs together, and while

113

she'll think I'm just being her friend, I'll just be using that time to ensure there are no surprises on the day of the race.

Then, when the race begins, she'll be the one who gets surprised because I won't be running the marathon next to her, chatting and keeping her company all the way around like I know many runners like to do with their own friends. No, I'll be off like a shot, leaving her for dust, and then she will know who I really am.

I'm running at a pace that is a little surprising even to me as I keep moving through the quiet streets. Perhaps it's because of all the alcohol in my system, fuelling me where I might have got tired if I was sober, but it's most likely just because I'm incredibly determined right now. Nothing can stop me. Not fatigue. Not an injury. Not the time of day or the fact that I've been drinking all night.

Nothing can stop me beating Lucy. It's inevitable.

And it's going to be a lot of fun when it happens.

19

LUCY

My head is pounding, my throat is dry, and my insides feel a little suspect, which all tells me one thing, as if I needed reminding.

I overdid it last night, and now I have to suffer the consequences.

Fortunately, I have come up with what I consider to be a relatively good hangover cure over the years. It's a combination of fizzy drinks and pills that can be purchased in the supermarket, and I already prepared both things before I went to sleep because I knew I wouldn't be in the mood for going far when I woke up.

Reaching out tentatively towards the bedside table, I pop a couple of pills from their packet before swallowing them down with a swig of the fizzy drink that will be my best friend today. Then I lie back and stare up at the ceiling, wondering if Jess is feeling as bad as I am today. I expect so because she matched me drink for drink, and she couldn't have got much more sleep than I did either. I decide to text my new friend and see how she is doing, figuring that a jokey message about the state of my condition will make her laugh and endear her to me some more.

I can hear Kirsty moving around in the flat as I type out my message to Jess, but I'm not in a rush to get up and go and see my flatmate. I'll catch up with her later when I'm feeling a little better. For now, I'm just going to lie here and try and distract myself from my predicament by scrolling around on my phone.

It takes me five minutes of reading a few news articles before I remember that I have the numbers of ten men saved on my device after last night's game with Jess. It almost feels like some kind of weird dream, but one check on my contacts list shows me that I did indeed make several new acquaintances last night, and I have the digits to prove it.

I cringe at what I must have looked like as I had gone around that bar and approached all those men. They must have thought I was so desperate to behave like that. But maybe some of them liked it. And maybe some of them are hoping that I will message them today.

Should I do so?

My first thought is not to do that because, frankly, I could do without the hassle of dating. But as I lie in my bed with my stinking hangover, I know I could use a little distraction. There wouldn't be any harm in sending one of these guys a text and seeing what he said back. I can just use it for my entertainment, a little bit of fun. I don't have to actually meet them.

But who would I text? I've got ten numbers to choose from, and I can't remember all the guy's names and faces, never mind tell them apart.

I'll just pick one that I like the sound of. Ryan. I guess that's a cool name. Let's see what Ryan is up to on this Saturday morning. Most probably lying in bed like I am, regretting his life choices from the previous evening.

'Hi, Ryan. It's Lucy from the bar last night. Just saying hi!'

I decide that will do for now. If and when he does message me back, I'll leave it to him to carry the weight in the conversation. I'm too tired to do the heavy lifting.

As I pass the time before Ryan might reply, I check to see if Jess has got back to my message yet. But she hasn't, and I figure that she's probably still sleeping.

Or maybe she has got up early to go for a run.

That's the moment I remember, to some horror, that I agreed to take part in a marathon with Jess next month.

What the hell was I thinking making a commitment like that? It's going to take some serious training to get ready for such a thing, and while I am fit and certainly have the drive and determination to complete several gruelling training runs, it's going to eat up quite a lot of my free time outside of work.

But I can't back out now. Not after I gave my word to Jess. That would make it look like I chickened out, and I don't want her to think I'm like that. She's the first person I've ever met that has a sliver of the competitive spirit I do.

I wonder if she is out running now, getting a jump start on her training, but it's unlikely. It's still early. She'll be sleeping. She's competitive, but she's not a machine.

I am looking forward to seeing her again, and as I think about her and all the things she told me last night, I find myself navigating to her company's website. I can remember the name of it, which is one of the few things I can remember about the prior night's events, and I'm curious to see if there is a bio page on the website in which it lists the staff who work there. Sure enough, I find that there is, and I only have to scroll down the page a little bit to find Jess's part. There is a photo of her with her arms crossed and looking a little imposing beside her name, job title and work email address.

I browse around the rest of the website out of interest, curious because I figure any company that can keep Jess happy and motivated must be a good one to work at. There are plenty of accolades and awards listed on the homepage of the website, all prestigious prizes that this company has won over the years thanks to the hard work of its employees, and it really does seem like it's a leader in its field.

Then I spot a word on the drop-down menu that makes me even more curious.

Vacancies.

I click the word out of interest, just to see what positions might be available here, not that I'm planning on sending in my CV. Well, not unless there's something very appealing anyway.

The first position is for the title of 'Global Strategic Manager,' and while that does sound good, especially the salary figure that goes with it, I know that is a little out of my league. But then I see there is a vacant position for 'Sales Account Manager', and that intrigues me because I know that is Jess's job title too. There's an opening in her department, and because of

118

that, I can now see exactly how much money she makes by reading the job description.

The figure I find is not actually as impressive as I would have thought, but it does say that bonuses are a big part of the position, and I recall Jess saying as such. It does sound very much like recruitment, I suppose. Just a different industry.

Something new.

Something challenging.

Should I apply for this role? It wouldn't do any harm to submit my CV, I guess. It's not as if I'm desperate for a job. I already have a good one, and I'm doing fine for money, so it won't be the end of the world if they don't get back to me. But I am definitely in need of a change, and this might be it. Perhaps it was fate that I met Jess because it has led me to this website and this job vacancy. I'm not such a big believer in luck, preferring more concrete words like 'hard work' and 'focused intention', but who knows how this mysterious world we live in really works?

If fate is a thing, I really should apply.

I decide I'll think about it for a little while, plus being hungover is probably not the best time to be applying for jobs, so I come off the website for the time being and check my messages again to see if Jess has got back to me. She hasn't, but there is a new message waiting, and it's from Ryan.

Let's see what he has got to say.

'Hey, you. I'll admit I was wondering if you would message or not. Nice to hear from you. Did you have a good night?'

119

It's a short, simple and polite message, and he has asked me a question, indicating that he is happy to start some discourse and see where it leads us. Normally, I'd be far too busy to be entertaining a whimsical thing like this that will probably lead nowhere, but seeing as I'm in such a bad way and unlikely to do anything but lie in my bed all day feeling sorry for myself, I might as well humour him and pass the time by replying.

It's not as if Jess has got back to me yet either.

20

It's been a week since my night out with Lucy, and we've met up a couple of times since then for training runs ahead of the marathon that we have both now entered. It wasn't difficult for either of us to reserve our places in the 26.2 mile test of endurance because, unlike the big city events where participants need to raise a certain amount of sponsorship for charity to even be considered, this one is open to anyone who fancies the challenge.

Having submitted our entries, the pair of us received our race numbers by email. They are the numbers that will be emblazoned across the front of our vests on race day, and they are also the numbers that will be beside all the final times that get posted onto the marathon's website page when it's all over.

I can't wait to see my number ranked much higher than Lucy's.

With our entries in, training could commence in earnest, although unbeknownst to the woman I am running the marathon with, my training had started earlier. I ended up running over ten miles in the early hours of the morning after I had got home from my first meeting with Lucy, and I have made sure to run at least that same distance every day since then too. I'll increase my miles as we get closer to the big day, but I've already made a solid start, and I know that I'm way ahead of

121

Lucy. I know that because she not only told me as much, but I could tell when we went out running together a couple of days ago.

I was making sure to go slow as the pair of us set off around the park in the centre of town, a park that will feature in the marathon and, on the day, will be filled with hundreds of people who have come out to support all the runners. I didn't want Lucy to know that I was fitter than I seemed because that might have made her increase her own training in her spare time. But we had only been going for around fifteen minutes when Lucy admitted she wasn't as fit as she could be and that she needed to slow down a little.

I was surprised by her admission because I would never have shown such weakness in front of her, but it was another sign that she was starting to see me more as a friend than a rival these days. That will be her downfall, but for the time being, I will play along with it, and I made sure to do so that day in the park.

I agreed that we could slow down, pretending like I was sympathetic, as well as a little out of breath myself, even though I felt like I could run for miles without tiring. It was as we slowed the pace and spent more time walking rather than running that Lucy and I got to know each other more, and she told me about a current problem she had at work with a client, as well as how she was having to make herself scarce from her flat again soon because her flatmate, Kirsty, was having a guy around again.

It was all boring, non-consequential stuff, but I humoured her and made sure to chip in with some sentences of my own to make it seem like I was listening and engaged with what she was saying. But I spent most of the time just visualising what it would be like to finish the marathon well ahead of her and seeing the look on her face when I tell her that instead of being my friend, she is just an opponent to me.

An opponent that will soon be vanquished and left on a scrapheap in my past as I move on to the next challenge.

I have another training run scheduled with Lucy tomorrow, but for now, I am focused on work as I walk into my office and stroll past the receptionist. I'm not very chatty with the woman that is stationed at the front desk of this building, even though we're technically colleagues and see each other every weekday. That's a conscious decision. The last thing I need is somebody else in my life sucking up all my free time with offers to go for drinks or worse, a 'brunch.' Women my age waste so much of their time doing silly things like that. If the receptionist spent less time eating brunch on her weekends and more time figuring out how to improve her skills, then she might stand a chance at getting out from behind that desk and up to the fifth floor where the real talent in this office works.

I ride the lift all the way up to where my desk awaits me but stop by in the kitchen before I get there to make myself a small protein shake. This supplement is one I have started taking to help me with the upcoming marathon, and according to all the online 'Running' forums that I have read extensively, it's the best one to take in the build-up to the big day. I'm going to leave no stone unturned as I attempt to get myself in the best shape I can be in for the race, and as I mix my drink, I smile at my dedication and commitment to everything I set my mind to.

I really am quite special, which is what made Lucy's 98% comment so galling.

With my drink made and ready to be consumed from the comfort of my chair at my desk, I leave the kitchen, but what I see waiting for me out in the corridor is almost enough to cause me to drop my drink all over the floor.

I see Greg, my boss, walking with a woman in a smart white blouse and black suit trousers.

But it's not just any woman.

It's Lucy.

I have absolutely no idea what she is doing here, but I am sure as hell going to find out, so I rush after them before they can disappear into one of the meeting rooms.

'Lucy?' I say as Greg opens a door for her, and the pair of them spin around to see me coming towards them.

'Oh, hi, Jess,' Lucy replies. 'I was wondering if I would see you. I've just been telling Greg how I know you.'

She smiles at me then, as does Greg, but I'm not smiling. I'm still trying to figure out what is going on.

'Why are you here?' I ask, not in a rude manner but a very blunt one, nonetheless.

'Lucy is here for a job interview,' Greg tells me then. 'And we're running a little behind, so if you don't mind, I'm sure you two can catch up later. Lucy, after you.'

Greg holds out his hand to show that he is letting Lucy into the meeting room ahead of him like a gentleman, and she smiles before mouthing 'Bye' to me and going inside.

I remain standing in the corridor and stare at the door as it closes behind Greg, trying to process what I have just heard.

Lucy has applied for a job here?

I can't believe it. Why the hell would she have done such a thing? The obvious answer is that she wants to work in this place. But why?

Because I'm here?

I remember that she showed a lot of interest in my job and where I worked back when we first met, and I was certainly informative with my answers because I wanted to really sell myself and impress her with my professional prowess. But I had never known that being so open would have led to her wanting to come and work in the same place that I do.

She did mention how she was thinking about making a change and seeking a new challenge after a couple of drinks that fateful Friday night in the bar, so I guess this is how she is going about it. But will it work? Will she get the job here? Is Greg going to like her enough to give her a chance? If he does then Lucy will be my team because that is where the vacancy lies. If so, we will be competing for the same clients and the same bonuses. That will mean Lucy isn't just my rival in

125

my personal life, but she will be my rival professionally too.

As I walk away from the meeting room with my protein shake in hand, I try to figure out if I want Lucy to be successful and get the job here. But by the time I reach my desk, I have come up with an answer.

I do want her to get it.

After all, any extra chance I can get to destroy her is a welcome one.

21

LUCY

There are not many things in life that can make you feel more validated than somebody offering you a job. That moment they reach across the table to shake your hand and tell you that you're hired is always an exhilarating one because it proves that you possess skills that somebody else covets. I know I should be old enough now not to seek the approval of others, but there's no denying it still felt good to hear Greg tell me that he wanted me to join his company.

As I walk out of the meeting room where the successful interview just took place, I'm hoping I'll bump into Jess again because then I could tell her the good news.

We're not just going to be friends.

We're going to be colleagues too.

In my mind, that is a great thing because it means our times together aren't just going to be the occasional training run for the marathon or one Friday night a month in a wine bar. We can go for lunch together every weekday. We could commute in and out of the office together. And if I'm lucky with the position of my new desk, we can talk to each other easily as we work.

This promises to be a lot of fun, although that is not the main reason I wanted to work here. As I told Greg in the interview, I am seeking a fresh challenge, and I'm doing that because I am not only ambitious but because I feel I have only just scratched the surface of what I can achieve in my current job. I believe that everything I do can grow exponentially if I'm in the right environment for it, and right here in this office seems like the perfect environment for me.

I keep a look out for Jess as I make my way back to the lifts on the fifth floor, but I don't see her. I suspect she's in an important meeting somewhere, already working hard on making today a successful one. No bother, I'll just make sure to call her later and pass on my news, unless, of course, her boss tells her it first.

I'll admit I was a little worried when Jess saw me going into the meeting room with Greg because I wasn't sure if it would distract him and make him question whether I was really here for the right reasons. I'd already been honest with him when he first met me in the reception area before my interview began, admitting that I first heard about his company because he already employs one of my friends. But he didn't seem to mind that, nor did he seem to mind when that friend interrupted us as we made our way into the meeting room.

In hindsight, it seemed to be Jess who was more surprised than Greg.

Perhaps I should have told my friend that I was trying to get a job here before she saw me walking around in her workplace. I'm sure she wouldn't have cared, and if anything, she most likely could have given me some tips to help me gain favour with Greg even quicker than I managed on my own. But I didn't tell her, and the main reason for that was because I was worried I wouldn't get this job, and then it might have made things a little awkward between us going forward. Jess wouldn't have felt as comfortable talking about her work and whatever bonus she might have been lucky enough to get if she knew that I had wanted to work there too. And for me, I would have struggled to stay positive about my own work situation if Jess knew I'd been trying to change it. That's why I thought I'd keep my application a secret, and if it didn't work out then nobody ever had to know.

But it has worked out, and I'll be starting my new job once I've served my notice period, which thankfully isn't long. Then I can sink my teeth into a new role, one that will push me and force me to grow rather than just keep coasting along doing something I've already proven myself capable of.

I treat myself to a cake and a coffee from the café around the corner from where my successful interview just took place, not in any rush to get back to my current workplace after pretending to them that I had a doctor's appointment to attend this morning. I know my colleagues will be surprised to learn that I am leaving when I tell them. Eight years is a long time to work in one place. But meeting Jess has really opened my eyes to the opportunity that is out there for me if I'm only willing to go looking for it. Her drive and determination really is an inspiration, and I cannot wait to not only see more of her but pick her brains about things, whether it's how to succeed under Greg or simply how she stays motivated all the time because while I'm very self-driven, she seems to be even better.

I think about texting her now to let her know the news, but I know she'll be busy, so I'll wait a while. But there is somebody else I can message to pass the time as I sit here and nibble on my cupcake. It's Ryan, the guy I have been messaging quite a lot ever since he was one of ten guys who gave me his number.

What started out as me seeking a little entertainment as I lay in bed dying from a hangover has developed into the two of us messaging back and forth to the point where he has asked me out on a date this weekend. He sent me the invite last night but a little shamefully, I haven't replied to him yet. I'm not being mean, I just didn't know what to say. But it's not fair to leave him hanging like this, so I will get back to him now.

The reason I didn't text him back when I first read his message was because I felt like going on a date wasn't something I wanted to do, but I didn't want to disappoint him immediately. I would have been quite happy just to keep texting each other for a while because it's fun, it's easy, and best of all, it's not time-consuming. But dating is time-consuming, and is that time I really have to spare right now? I'm going to be busy with my new job, and I'm certainly going to be putting in plenty of overtime to impress my new employer, so I'm not sure how I'd be able to fit Ryan in. It's best if I just let him down gently, saying that dating is not something I'm ready for at the moment. If he presses me, I could always just say I've come out of a long relationship and need a break from it all.

But just before I can type out my reply to him, I see a new message come through. He has sent me a funny selfie of himself on a train with what appears to be another man sleeping on his shoulder.

'My commute today. Great fun!'

I laugh at the message and the expression on Ryan's face in the image as he sits there in his suit with the stranger's head on him before I send him back a couple of emojis to let him know that I find it funny. But now I feel bad to change the mood of this chat by telling him I don't wish to meet him for a date. His message last night simply suggested a coffee somewhere, so I guess I could fit that in. Just one coffee. It doesn't have to lead to anything. Then I can get right back to focusing on what's more important to me, like getting ready for my new job and training for the marathon with Jess.

22

JESS

It's a lung-busting, stomach-churning run up the hill near my home, but it's a damn good view from the top when I get there. It feels even better once I've got my breath back and assured myself that I'm not going to have a heart attack because I know I have just put in some solid work that will pay dividends when the marathon comes around.

With my hands on my hips, I stare out across my town, knowing full well that Lucy is out there somewhere right now, possibly doing the same thing as me. Training. Working hard. Trying to get an edge. It's that thought that got me up this hill, and it's the same thought that will see me return to the bottom of it before forcing myself all the way up again.

I pass a couple of mothers chattering away as they push their babies up the hill in their prams, getting some exercise but nowhere near as much as I am getting today. I feel smug as I move past them, as if I'm superior because I'm running this hill while they are walking it. I'm ahead of them in terms of fitness, and that matters to me, even if they are complete strangers.

I'm in competition with everyone, whether they know it or not.

But it's the thought of the person I'm in competition with the most that returns to me as I get back to the bottom of the hill and turn around, trying to summon up the strength to run up it again.

Lucy.

I still don't know how her job interview with Greg went.

I didn't see her when she came out of that meeting room because I was busy in my own meeting elsewhere, but I did ask Greg when I saw him later that day. But he was coy and told me that he would update me and the rest of the staff with any personnel changes when he deemed fit. I thought that was a slightly odd thing to say, but I also took it as him saying that he had offered Lucy the job, and he was just waiting for the formalities to be taken care of before he made it official.

Of course, I could get confirmation by texting Lucy and asking her outright, but I fear that would make me look a little needy, as if I just have to know what she is doing. I don't need to know. I just need to focus on what I am doing. That's why I start running again, putting one foot in front of the other as I go up the steep incline, chasing down the backs of the two pram-pushers ahead of me.

I get a burst of speed on as I pass the mums again, and I wonder if they are marvelling at my endurance levels as they see me race past. But I don't turn around to look at them. I just keep my eyes on the top of the hill while replaying one of my favourite quotes in my head.

"Losers focus on winners. Winners focus on winning."

Having made it to the top again and feeling the exhilaration from the rush of endorphins coursing through my body, I decide to take a photo of the view so I can look back on it when I'm at home later. But that's when I notice I have a missed call from Lucy.

She tried me a minute ago, but I obviously missed it while I was putting my body through its paces, so I call her back to see what she wanted.

'Hey!' Lucy says when she answers, the cheery lilt to her voice letting me know that she is in a good mood, which only serves to irritate me for no reason.

'Hi. Sorry, I missed your call,' I say, whilst doing my best not to sound breathless so Lucy won't suspect I've been training hard without her.

'No problem! I was just giving you a ring to let you know how I got on with the job interview. I tried to find you when it finished, but I couldn't see you anywhere.'

'Oh, okay. How did it go?'

'Yeah, it was alright,' she admits, but her voice doesn't sound quite so cheery now.

In my head, I'm already preparing what I will say to her to console her. I'll tell her not to worry that it didn't go as she had hoped before I'll make a joke about it not being that great of a place to work anyway and how she has had a lucky escape. But secretly, I'll be delighted that she failed to make the grade, and she might even be able to pick up on a little of my happiness if she listens carefully to the tone of my voice as I'm listening to hers.

'What happened?' I ask her, expecting to hear some long-winded story about how the interview wasn't quite what she expected or about how she messed up answering one of Greg's questions and ruined her chances of impressing him. I'm rather amused by the thought of her stumbling over her sentences as she tried to tell him what her biggest strengths and weaknesses are.

'Well, it started well enough,' Lucy admits. 'We talked about my current role and the kind of skills I could bring.'

'That sounds good,' I say while smiling as I wait for the bad part.

'Yeah, I thought so too. And then he asked me some mock questions, like hypothetical problems I would have to solve if I was to work for him.'

'Ahhh yes, he did that with me in my interview. He does like a hypothetical question,' I say as I watch the two mums finally join me at the top of this hill with their babies.

'But then he told me that I had a problem,' Lucy says, and I really am grinning now.

'Oh. And what was that?'

I can't wait to hear it. I bet it's a good one.

'He told me that I had a problem in how I was going to break the news to my current employer that I was going to leave them and go and work for him!'

It takes me a few seconds to process what Lucy has just said, but when I do, I feel like throwing my phone off this hilltop.

I don't believe it. She got the job?

135

'I got the job!' Lucy squeals down the line, almost deafening me. 'We're going to work together! How cool! We can go for lunches and drinks after work!'

I still haven't said anything yet, and I'm not sure if I can. That's because this woman really is becoming a problem.

'Wow, well done,' I manage to muster as I watch one of the mums taking her baby out of the pram.

'Thanks!'

'So when do you start?'

'Soon! I've just got to serve my notice, but Greg seemed pretty keen on getting me in as quickly as possible. It sounds like he has big plans for the company.'

I already know he has big plans for the company, and I was banking on being the one to bring much of it to fruition for him, ensuring that my bonuses only grew larger as time went on. But now there's a new member in my team, how is that going to affect my earning potential? I know I can beat every other one of my colleagues in sales. But can I beat Lucy?

'That's great,' I say before feeling the urgent need to wrap this conversation up. 'Look, I'm sorry, but I've got to go as I'm in the middle of something. But we'll speak soon, okay?'

'Sure, no problem! We'll get a date in to go for a run!'

'Yeah, okay. Bye.'

I can't hang up quickly enough, but once I have, I still want to throw my phone down this hill. But that

136

isn't sensible, so I do the only other thing I can, which is start walking back down it again. I was going to go home soon, but after that call, I'm going to run up this hill several more times before I have a rest.

But just before I start descending again, I pass the mother holding her baby out of her pram, and when I do, my bad mood gets the better of me, and I have to make a comment on the child's appearance, if only to make someone else feel as bad as I feel right now.

'That's one ugly baby,' I say to the smiling mother. 'Just like it's mother.'

23

LUCY

First days are always nerve-wracking. I remember my first day at school when I wouldn't let go of my mother's hand and begged her not to make me go through the gates with all those strangers. I remember my first day at university when I had to figure out how to live away from home by myself. And I remember my first day at the recruitment agency where I would go on to stay for eight years, trying to remember everybody's name and not wanting to make a mistake that would see me fall straight back into the unemployment pool again.

Now it's time for another first day because I'm here to start work trying to obtain more clients for this office renovation company. Greg has already welcomed me in and shown me around, introducing me to several of my new colleagues as well as giving me all the important information like where the toilets are located and how the coffee machine works. Now the pleasantries are over, I'm sitting at my desk and am ready to log in with the credentials that HR have given me so I can begin looking through my inbox and forming a plan as to how I am best going to tackle this new challenge. But before I do that, I decide to check in with Jess because, as I had hoped, she isn't sitting too far away from me in this office.

She's not too far away at all.

Her desk is opposite mine, and I can see her if I just move my head slightly to the left or right and look around my bulky computer screen. I do just that and see Jess with her phone to her ear as she writes something down on a piece of paper.

I won't interrupt her call. She's busy, as she has been all morning. She's been so busy that she hasn't had too much time for conversation, although she did wish me luck when I sat down at my desk. She also told me not to demand too much of myself because this industry is different to the last one that I worked in, and I shouldn't get too down on myself if I don't see immediate success.

It was nice of her to give me advice and show some concern, even if it would also have been nice for her to have a little more confidence in me than that and not just assume that I'm going to take a while to get up and running here. I'm certainly not planning on taking things slowly or lowering the ambitions that drove me to apply for a job here in the first place. I want to show Greg that he made the right choice in hiring me, and I also want to show the rest of the sales team, including Jess, that I am worthy of being a part of it. Just because Jess is a friend, it doesn't mean that I'm not going to try my best to achieve bigger sales figures than her and claim the bonuses that she seems to win every month. I'm going to work hard to prove myself, and I just hope that Jess understands it's nothing personal.

This is business, and we can still be friendly outside of that.

Jess ends her call a moment later, and I take the opportunity to ask her how her morning is going.

'Yeah, it's fine,' she tells me as she keeps her eyes on her screen and types something on her keyboard.

'Got any meetings today?'

'One this afternoon.'

'Cool. Big client?'

'Potentially.'

'Nice. Who are they?'

'I'm sorry, I've just got to get this email out. We'll chat at lunch, okay?'

'Oh, okay. Sure. Sorry.'

I leave Jess to get on with whatever she is doing, slightly stung at how she dismissed me as I tried to make conversation. But I get it. She didn't get to the strong position she was in by chatting all day. She works hard and gets results, and that's what I need to be doing if I'm to compete with her come the next round of bonus meetings.

I spend the rest of the morning learning how to navigate my way around the company's internal systems while listening to Jess make several calls on her phone. It's obvious, even at this early stage, why she is outperforming everyone else at these other desks. It's because she just grinds. The other members of the team are in and out of their seats going to the kitchen or the bathroom or chatting by the water cooler for several minutes out of every hour. But Jess just hustles, and the only time she has gotten up out of her seat has been when she has taken a few calls on her work mobile.

At first, I was worrying that she was deliberately taking the calls elsewhere because she didn't want me to hear who she was talking to or what she was talking about in case I tried to steal her clients and ideas. But I'm sure that's just a little silly paranoia on my part and not the case. Even if she was worried about a little friendly competition, I doubt she would be worried already.

It's getting close to lunchtime, and I'm looking forward to Jess showing me one of the local places she likes to grab food at shortly, but before that, Greg approaches me at my desk and asks me if he can have a word with me in private. I instantly worry that I have already done something wrong and that he is going to tell me to pack up my things and leave, but I'm not sure what it is that I could have done because I haven't been here long enough to make any mistakes. But then we reach his office, and after he has closed the door, he tells me what is on his mind.

He is considering targeting a whole new set of clients; clients that his company have never gone after before. The reason he is telling me about it and not anybody else is because he wants me to be the lead sales rep on it.

I ask him why me and not one of my other more experienced colleagues, and while I don't mention Jess by name, that is exactly who I am referring to. But he tells me that I have an advantage over them, and it is that I'm not used to the traditions and routines that come in this industry. He wants someone who can approach this project with a fresh pair of eyes, rather than someone who has been doing this for years and will fall back on old habits.

That makes sense to me, I suppose, although I worry a little that it might not go down so well with the rest of my team who might feel like I have come in and made myself the boss's pet, someone who has essentially skipped the line and got myself ahead. But it doesn't have to be like that. I'm just doing whatever the boss tells me to do, and I know they would do the same. And if they don't like it, they could always look elsewhere for a fresh challenge, just like I have done. There has to be some reward for people like me who take a risk and move companies, rather than being one of those who stays at the same place forever, never venturing out of their comfort zone and, therefore, never growing.

I feel excited about the new project lying ahead of me as I return to my desk, but I've barely sat down before Jess asks me what my meeting with Greg was all about. I let her know that I'll tell her at lunch, but I only say that because I don't want anyone else overhearing.

Jess seems a little perturbed by that, but it's no different to when she dismissed me earlier and told me to wait until we were on our break. But lunchtime should be fun. We have lots to talk about, and it's only day one of me being here.

24

JESS

It's only day one of Lucy being here, and she has already got something I was never able to get in all the time I have worked in my job. She has a special project to work on with Greg rather than just the general projects that everyone else works on.

How has she managed that?

'He said I would be best for it because I was new,' Lucy tells me as we stand in line at the salad bar that I like to come to when I'm eating healthily, which is most of the time but especially now I am in training for a marathon.

I suspect she has just told me that to try and make it seem less likely she is being given this task unfairly, but there's nothing she could say that wouldn't make me frustrated by this turn of events. All the years I've worked for Greg and never been offered a chance like this while Lucy swans into the office on her first day and the opportunity falls at her feet.

I suppose I could try and be content with just hoping that she fails in her new task because that will be the quickest way for Greg to lose his enthusiasm for her. But I'm never content with the passive option, and it would certainly be passive of me to just sit around and hope for Lucy to make a mess of things. I will have to actively do whatever I can to disrupt her progress, secretly, of course, as a way of not only ensuring her demise at this company but speeding it up as well. All while pretending to be her friend. It's not going to be easy, but I live for the challenges in this world.

'I'll get lunch today,' Lucy tells me as we shuffle further forward in the queue. 'It can be my way of thanking you.'

'Thanking me? For what?'

'If you hadn't messaged me then we would never have met, and I would never have this incredible new job now.'

It annoys me how true that is, but I do well not to show it before Lucy goes on.

'I know it's only a salad, but I'll buy you a drink the next time we're out.'

'You don't have to do that.'

'I know, but I want to.'

Lucy is being very nice to me, not that it is going to detract from how much I am looking forward to showing her that she is not on my level.

'So, what do you recommend?' Lucy asks me as we reach the counter and peruse the array of green, leafy options before us.

'The Deluxe Salad is good,' I say, referring to the £10 salad that I have tried once before but tend not to get too often because of how pricey it is.

I deliberately picked that one because it's expensive, and I want Lucy to have to spend as much as possible if she feels like she wants to buy me something.

'Oh, okay,' she says, having clearly clocked the price tag. 'Is that what you want?'

'Yes.'

'Cool. Two Deluxe Salads then please.'

The woman behind the counter gets to work putting our two salad trays into a paper bag, and I stand aside as Lucy pays for them. Then we take our seats at one of the tables and tuck into our healthy lunch alongside all the other employees that are packed into here after parting with a little of the wages that they have spent all morning working so hard to earn.

I'm hoping that Lucy isn't going to try and ask me for any tips on how to perform well in this industry or ways to impress Greg in meetings because I don't want to have to do anything that might help her. That was why I kept leaving my desk whenever one of my bigger clients called me. I didn't want her eavesdropping and figuring out my formula to success. But she doesn't bring up work. Instead, she starts to tell me about some guy called Ryan.

'I only started messaging him because I was bored,' she admits through a mouthful of lettuce. 'And I randomly selected his number from the ten we got in the bar that night. Like a lucky dip.'

'Wait, you actually messaged one of those guys?'

'Yeah.'

'But it was only a game.'

'I know, but like I said, I was bored. I didn't think it would lead to anything. But we've actually been getting on pretty well, and we've met a couple of times now.'

It's not that I'm jealous of Lucy and her new love interest because I'm not. I have far more important things to busy myself with than matters of the heart. It's just I'm wondering how she is managing to fit all of this in amongst starting a new job and training for the marathon. Unless she hasn't been training as hard for the marathon as I have, which would be good on one hand because it would mean I have even more of a chance of finishing ahead of her, but it would be bad on the other because I want to know she has done her absolute best. That way, it will sting her even more when she sees that it was still nowhere near good enough.

But she's dating now, which leads me to worry that she might be distracted, and that's no good. I have to know that she wants to beat me as much as I want to beat her. But all this friendly chat is starting to get me worried that she doesn't care as much as I thought she did when I first met her.

'We're meeting up again one night this week,' she tells me as she keeps on eating while I just pick at my meal. 'We've got a table at that tapas place on Brook Street. It's got great reviews.'

I nod my head while I continue to stab my plastic fork into my leafy meal.

'I'm not really sure if it's going to go anywhere, and I expect I'll be too busy to even think about having a proper relationship now I have this new project to work on for Greg,' Lucy admits. 'But I've been off the dating scene for so long that I'll admit it has been quite nice to have a little male attention again. Plus, it gives me someone to go and see if my flatmate kicks me out again.'

I nod again, only half-listening and more focused on stabbing the small lentil that is at the bottom of my tray, if only because I'm imagining it is Lucy's eyeball.

'So, what about you? How's your love life?'

I manage to get the lentil and stare at it, skewered on my fork, before I brush her question off and make a point of checking the time.

'I really should get going. I need to prepare for my meeting this afternoon, and I've just remembered there's something I haven't done for it.'

'But you've hardly touched your salad!'

'It's okay, I'll take it with me. I might have it for my dinner tonight. Shall I see you back at the office?'

I stand up to leave, hoping that Lucy will stay here and finish eating alone, which she does, telling me she will see me later and wishing me luck for my meeting. That forces me to give her a fake smile before I walk away, eager to get away from her and her boring tales of Ryan.

The first thing I do when I get out of the salad bar is put my sunglasses on because the clouds have parted, and it's a lot brighter than it was when I first went inside.

The second thing I do is toss the salad into the nearest bin I can find.

25

LUCY

I've only been in my new job three days, but I'm already making inroads into my new challenge. Wanting to impress Greg as quickly as possible, I have spent every possible minute I can either working at my desk or thinking up ways to find new clients as I've been commuting, running or lying in my bed. Because of that dedication to my new task, I have made progress, and now I'm putting the finishing touches on the report I am going to send Greg to show him what I have planned.

I'm not letting the fact that it is seven o'clock in the evening deter me from my work, ignoring all the other empty desks around this deserted office as I keep working while everyone else enjoys their leisure time. Nor am I going to let the fact that I was supposed to be on a date with Ryan tonight distract me or make me feel bad for letting him down.

It is a shame that I had to cancel on him, but I explained why and he understood, or at least I hope he did, for his sake more than mine. I hope he understood because if he is the kind of guy who would rather I put a trip to the cinema ahead of my ambitions in the workplace then I wouldn't want to see him again anyway. There will always be time to catch a movie, but I only get one chance at impressing Greg in the early part of my tenure here, and I'm not going to screw that up by trading hard work for popcorn.

Ryan did seem to take it fairly well, texting me to say that we would just rearrange, and I appreciated that before putting my phone away to carry on with my work. Now I've been focused on it so much that I hadn't realised it was getting so late, and I should probably leave this office soon, or I might risk being locked in here all night. But I don't want to stop working yet. There is too much to do, and besides, my competitive juices are flowing again, and once that is the case, there is no stopping me.

I'm competing against everyone else in my team, all those who aren't here right now working as hard as me. That includes Jess, though I suspect it will take me a while to outperform her seeing as she already had such a head start here. But I have the feeling that she is worried, and while we are still friends, I have detected a slight change in her demeanour with me this week. I first picked up on it when she left me early at the salad bar, bringing an abrupt end to our lunch break and rushing back to work on something when I'm convinced she could have stayed and sat with me a little longer. If I had to guess, I would say that she didn't take too well to the news that Greg has given me a special assignment. She's always been number one around here, and now there's a new player in town, not that I'm trying to rub it in her face. I really do want us to be friends, but we'll just have to see how that goes, especially if I start getting the better of her in the bonus meetings.

Thinking about Jess, I look over at her empty desk, and I'm still shocked that she finished so early today. She told me that she had a meeting at four o'clock at another office and that she wouldn't be coming back because there wouldn't be much point at that time. That made sense, but it surprised me that she didn't always work late, especially since I have already shown everyone else here that I'm not afraid of staying past five o'clock. But her desk is empty and unmanned, and while I suppose she could be working at home, that still doesn't beat being in the office.

I'm right in the middle of typing out a paragraph that will outline to Greg why I believe we can really capitalise on the clients he has already identified but aren't currently performing for him when nature calls and I have to get up to go to the bathroom. I grimace as I go because my legs have been aching a lot recently thanks to all the training runs I have been putting in for the upcoming marathon, the marathon that I know Jess is working hard for because I've seen her moving a little gingerly around the office too. The pair of us haven't been training together as much as I thought we would when she first suggested it, but as long as we are both on track to make it to the start line then I guess it doesn't matter.

I check my phone while I'm in the bathroom, and with the craziness of the last few days, I realise I haven't been on the app that I used to enjoy so much. I haven't been participating in any competitions with an unknown online user recently because I've had plenty to keep me occupied in the real world, but I decide to have a browse around on there just to see what I might have been missing out on. When I do, I notice that there are plenty of contests underway as usual, ranging from the simple to the downright crazy.

Wondering if Jess has found the time to participate in anything new recently, I go onto her profile for a snoop around. But just like me, she has been inactive, a result of which has seen her maintain her 99% win ratio. That number would have always caught my eye no matter whose profile I had seen it on, but now I have gotten to know Jess, it impresses me even more. That's because while I have seen glimpses of her competitive spirit, like the night she made me play the phone number game in the bar, I haven't seen too much else to show me that she is a woman that has to win at all costs.

Maybe she isn't so much competitive as she is fortunate, or maybe she has figured out how to work smart instead of just working hard. Whatever traits she possesses to have become so accustomed to winning, I feel like I am the one who is the better competitor. I have beaten her at everything we have done so far, after all, and I am confident I can outdo her both at work and in the marathon too.

As I leave the bathroom and make my way back to my desk, I'm planning on wrapping things up here in the next ten minutes or so then going home to see Kirsty. I might even call for a takeaway on the way back too, and I'll check with my flatmate to see if she wants to go halves on it with me. But then I see something that causes me to forget all about going home, having food and chilling out.

'Jess?' I say when I see my friend sitting at her desk.

'Lucy!' she replies, seeming just as surprised to see me as I am to see her.

'You scared me! I thought I was on my own!' I tell her with my hand over my chest and, more specifically, my racing heart.

'You scared me too! What are you still doing here?'

'I've been working. What about you? I thought you weren't coming back after your meeting?'

'I changed my mind.'

'Oh, I see.'

I wonder if Jess is really telling me the truth or if she has always been coming back to work here once she believes everyone has left. Have I got her all wrong? Has she secretly been outworking me while I thought I was outworking her? Does it matter? Maybe not to two regular people but to two competitive spirits like us, I guess it does.

That's why I change my mind about finishing up and going home for a takeaway. Instead, I sit back at my desk and carry on working, just like Jess does. We make small talk as we type, but neither one of us is overly chatty. But it's what is unsaid between us that seems to be the loudest thing.

It's the knowledge that neither one of us will want to be the first one to leave.

This could be a very long night.

25

JESS

It's time for another monthly sales meeting, and I'm looking forward to this even more than any of the previous ones. That's because this will be the first time that I have the opportunity to establish some genuine dominance over Lucy. She is sitting around this table now for the first time, waiting for Greg to run through his familiar routine, and I can tell she is a little nervous because she keeps fiddling with her pen and tapping it against her notepad.

I've been around her enough now to pick up on some of her 'tells', and because of that, I have a good sense of when she is feeling a certain way. She's as edgy as she was on her first day in her new job, but I haven't seen any of those nerves since then because she has settled in around here surprisingly well.

Until now.

Now she is nervous again, and I wonder why.

I'll admit that I am a little on edge, but that's only because I'm eager to know how much my bonus is this month. I'm expecting another big pay-out thanks to once again having the best sales figures on the team, so at least I have a reason to be anxious. But I'm not sure what Lucy has to worry about. She hasn't been here long enough to qualify for a bonus, so unless she just gets anxious in meetings in general, it's a little strange.

She hasn't noticed that I have been watching her yet, or at least I don't think she has, but this isn't the first time I've found myself distracted by her presence recently. How can I forget the night last week when Lucy and I ended up staying in the office until midnight, both of us working, or at least pretending to, as we tried to outlast the other one and not be the first one to go home?

It was weird how it became a competition considering that neither one of us actually admitted to it being so, but there's no doubt in my mind that it was. Just because we weren't playing a game on an app or in a bar, it didn't mean the gauntlet hadn't been thrown down. I had been determined not to leave my desk first, and Lucy had been the same. In the end, we had both been forced to leave when Winston, the security guard in charge of locking up the office, had come up to our floor to tell us that his shift was over and he wanted us out so he could set the alarm system. Therefore, it had ended in a draw between Lucy and I as we had logged off, put our coats on and made our way to the lift, and while a draw is better than another loss to her, it still wasn't the victory that I craved.

The pair of us had chatted in the lift on the way down to the ground floor, but neither one of us had acknowledged the elephant in the room, which was that we both knew what the other one had been trying to accomplish, and we had both been willing to go without a night's sleep to do it.

A psychologist would certainly have fun studying us two and trying to figure out why we are both so competitive, but neither of us would have the time to read whatever report they produced.

We'd simply be too busy trying to win at something else.

But after that long night in the office, it has become a little harder for me to keep Lucy thinking that I am just her friend. Admittedly, that is my fault because I'm not doing a very good job of keeping up appearances. I honestly thought I would be able to play nice with her until the marathon, where I planned on destroying her and laughing in her face, but then she joined my company, and now I'm around her every day, things are too hard. We still chat, and we still text but not as much, and I feel like Lucy knows I am holding something back when I am around her.

She knows that I still view her as a rival.

Interestingly though, she doesn't seem to care. She is still warm towards me, even after our late night in the office that turned into a tense standoff as we kept yawning and asking the other one when they were leaving. Is that because she thinks she has the measure of me? Does she think there's nothing to be afraid of and that she has me beat in anything?

If so, this meeting has come at just the right time because this is one battleground that I have never lost on. And I don't plan on changing that today.

I see Lucy's posture stiffen a little when the door opens and Greg walks in before she glances at me, and we make eye contact. But there's no time for anything to be said before our boss speaks and gets the meeting underway.

'Okay, first of all, I'd like to acknowledge the extra person we have around the table now,' Greg says as he smooths down the fabric on his gold-coloured tie. 'Lucy joined us just over a week ago. How have you found it so far?'

Greg looks towards Lucy, who smiles at him before answering.

'I've enjoyed it. Everyone's been very welcoming.'

'Good to hear, not that I expected anything less,' Greg says as he finally stops messing with his tie and lets his hands rest in his lap. 'It's good to have you on board with us. This team could use a little livening up.'

A few of my colleagues around the table chuckle, but I don't. I just want him to get on with it.

Tell me that I have the most impressive stats of the month, give me that big, juicy bonus, and most importantly, show Lucy that I am the top dog around here.

'Right, as everyone around this table already knows and as Lucy is about to find out, I don't like to waste time in these meetings,' Greg says as he leans forward in his seat and looks down at the piece of paper in front of him. 'So, without further ado, it's time to reveal who the top sales performer was this month.'

Here we go. Listen to this, Lucy. You've seen my 99% stat on the app, but around here, I'm 100%, and you're about to find out why.

'This month's biggest bonus is awarded to our newest member, Lucy.'

What?

156

I mustn't have heard Greg right there. He just said Lucy, but it can't be her. She's barely been here two minutes. There's no way she could have brought in more business than me.

'Well done, Lucy. It's not a bad start, is it?' Greg asks her, and Lucy thanks him as the rest of the team looks on in differing states of confusion. But Lucy doesn't seem confused. She seems comfortable, as if she already knew the result beforehand because Greg had told her or because she is just supremely confident in her ability to come in here and beat us all. I really hope it's the former and not the latter because that would be very disconcerting.

Thankfully, as I'm not the only one who is surprised by this turn of events, it gets questioned by the colleague to my right.

'Erm...well done, Lucy. Honestly. But can I just ask how she has managed to win despite only just starting here?'

The question posed to Greg is a very good one, and I wait with bated breath to hear the answer.

'Certainly,' he says as he leans back in his seat again and returns to stroking his tie. 'Some of you might not be aware, but I put Lucy on a special project when she started here. She was tasked with helping me grow the business in an area I had identified, and while I had expected that to take some time to bear fruit, it seems Lucy had other ideas. It was only yesterday when she secured her first client, and it wasn't just any old client. It was a seven-figure one. That's how she won, and that's why she's getting the biggest bonus.'

There it is. The truth. Greg wouldn't lie, after all. Lucy really must have brought more money into the business than any of us this month, and she did it all in much less time.

The rest of the meeting is a blur as sales figures are read out, and the rest of the bonuses are distributed. But none of them are at the level that Lucy got, and I'm almost embarrassed when it comes time for me to get mine.

When the meeting ends and everyone stands up, I just want to get out of the room as quickly as possible. But I end up arriving at the door at the same time as Lucy and when I do, I begrudgingly give her a 'congratulations' because what else can I do? Stomp my feet and say it isn't fair? I won't give her the pleasure.

But it's hard to keep quiet as she excitedly tells me how she has never received a bonus so large, and she plans to use some of the money on her upcoming date with Ryan at the new Italian restaurant on Clarkson Street. She's going on Saturday night, apparently, and she's heard good things about the menu. But I couldn't care less. She's just beaten me again, and now she's harping on about meatballs and spaghetti.

I eventually get away from her and lock myself in one of the cubicles in the ladies' bathroom to calm myself down before going back to my desk. But as I stand there sucking in several deep breaths and trying to comprehend how I could have suddenly gone from such a winner to such a loser, I know I can't stand for this. This woman is beating me at everything, and that marathon is still too far away. I need to beat her at something else before then, and if I've failed in the workplace, there's only one other way I can think of to get back at her.

It's a bold move, and it's unlike anything I've ever done before.

But I'm willing to do anything now.

I'll do whatever it takes to prove I am the better woman.

26

LUCY

Having already spent half an hour looking at this restaurant's menu online before I got here, I know what I want to order. But I don't want my date to think that I'm some kind of ravenous pig who reads menus on the internet, so I must pretend like I'm seeing this choice of dishes for the first time.

'The linguine sounds good,' I say, stroking my chin as if I am really pondering things.

'I'm tempted by the carbonara,' Ryan admits before quickly changing his mind. 'But I also fancy a pizza.'

'There's so much choice, isn't there?'

'Yeah, I can see why this place has got good reviews.'

'Me too.'

The conversation is fairly tame, but that's only because we're still in the early stages of dating, and both of us are trying to be polite and impress. I've never really been in a relationship long enough to get truly comfortable with another man, but I have heard other women's stories about what they do in front of their partners once they have become used to each other. Burping, for example, as well as a few other ways of expelling gas from the human body that are even less subtle. But we're a long way away from that as we sit here in our best clothes and peruse the menu as if we're two food critics on a television show.

'Pizza it is!' Ryan exclaims as he slams his menu shut before he can see something else to change his mind. 'What about you?'

'I think I'll go for the linguine,' I reply, sticking with my original choice, although I've already made a mental note to invite Kirsty here so I can sample more of this menu with someone else.

I could always ask Jess to come here too, I suppose, although I'm not sure if it will be awkward. I could tell she was shocked that I was the star of the sales meeting with Greg, and while I'm sure she wasn't the only one, the surprise had to hit her the hardest. She's always won the biggest bonus, but now I've come along and beat her at that too.

Perhaps I should let her beat me at something, just to make things a little less tense between us. It goes against all my instincts to do such a thing, but maybe I'm slowly but surely arriving at a point in my life when I'm realising that there is more to it than just trying to be better than someone else. Kirsty has been trying to tell me that for years, but I guess I just had to figure it out on my own. Or maybe it's the introduction of Ryan into my life that has led me to question a few things about my behaviour.

I never thought I'd choose to go on a date in a fancy restaurant and eat lots of calorific food rather than be out training for a marathon I have coming up so I can put in my best possible performance. But here I am.

161

Ryan seems to have charmed me. But I think I have charmed him too.

'I like your necklace,' he says as he notices the silver 'L' hanging just above my chest. 'It's cute.'

'Thanks. My flatmate got it for me for my last birthday.'

'Ahhh, the infamous flatmate. I wonder if I'll ever get to meet her. I've heard so many stories.'

'You want to meet her?'

'Yeah, she's your best friend, isn't she?'

'Yep.'

'Then, sure.'

I smile because it's sweet that Ryan wants to get to know my best friend. Then again, he could just be saying anything to get himself back to my place, the sly dog.

'So, how's your week been?' Ryan asks me once we have placed our order with the nervous waiter who might be currently enduring his first ever shift in this industry.

'It's been good. Great, actually.'

'Oh yeah, how so?'

I deliberate internally for a moment as to whether or not I should tell Ryan about my bonus, but I decide that I should because I worked damn hard to get it, and there's no reason to shy away from it.

'I found out I was the top sales performer in my team,' I tell him with a proud smile.

'Really? That's great! Didn't you just start there?'

'Yeah, I've not been there long.'

'Wow, that's awesome! Well done to you.'

He holds his glass of wine across the table, and I clink mine against it as we toast to my success. It feels good to be able to truly enjoy it without feeling guilty. I wish Jess had been a little more sincere when she had congratulated me, but never mind.

'So, I guess dinner is on you tonight then,' Ryan teases me, but I just laugh and tell him that he'll never get to meet my flatmate with that kind of talk.

By the time our food comes, both of us are a lot more relaxed than when we first sat down and now this is yet another date of ours that is going well. I really like Ryan. He's funny, a good conversationalist once he has got past his initial nerves, and it doesn't hurt that he looks cute in a shirt.

Who knows? Maybe tonight will be the night I invite him back to meet Kirsty.

There is just one problem with that plan though, or there is if he ends up staying overnight. I am supposed to be up early for a training run with Jess in the morning. We scheduled it for seven AM, but that was before I had come out here, had a great time with Ryan, and got started on my third glass of wine. Suddenly, that early morning run doesn't seem quite as appealing.

I guess I could text her to cancel. But what will she think of me if I do that? That I'm lazy? Undisciplined? Unfocused? I don't want that. I could just pretend that I'm ill. A headache or stomach bug might get me off the hook. She might buy that, and while she'll probably feel disappointed that I've let her down, she can still go for the run by herself. She doesn't need me alongside her to keep her motivated. She seems to manage that well enough on her own.

I've decided it as I finish my main meal and entertain Ryan's idea of looking at the dessert menu. I'm going to text Jess and let her know that I won't be running in the morning. It's not like me to have chosen a fun night and a lie-in over being productive, but at this moment, that's what I'd rather do.

I'm sure Jess won't mind.

She's probably out having fun herself somewhere tonight too.

27

JESS

Lucy was right. This Italian restaurant does look nice. It's a shame I won't be sampling any of the food prepared inside it this evening. I'll have to make do with being out here across the street, just watching the windows and, more specifically, watching Lucy eating her dessert with her date.

I've been watching the pair ever since I saw them arrive at the time and place Lucy had told me they would be arriving at. Of course, when she mentioned her exciting Saturday night date to me in the office the other day, she won't have imagined that I would be using that information to spy on her. But as long as she continues to underestimate me then I have a chance at beating her at something.

The cold wind blowing out on this street is stinging my face, but it doesn't sting half as much as the pain I felt when Lucy beat me in my own backyard. She's already Greg's favourite, despite everything I have done for him over the years. I can tell that because he doesn't talk to me half as much as he talks to her now. She's the one who gets all the one-to-one meetings that I used to get, and she's the one he talks about most proudly in the team meetings.

That bitch is taking everything from me. My status at work. My winning streaks. My pride. Everything.

That's why it's time I took something off her.

Lucy is now looking at her mobile phone, and while I consider that to be bad table manners while she is eating with someone else, I find out what she was doing on it a moment later when I receive a text message. It's from her.

'Hi, Jess. So sorry, but I won't be able to make it for our training run tomorrow morning. I'm not feeling well, so an early run probably isn't the best thing for me right now. I'll hopefully see you at work on Monday xx'

The bare-faced lie from Lucy is a poor one and not only because I can see her sitting in a restaurant now instead of lying at home on her sickbed. It's poor because she must know that it's very out of character to bail out of a commitment like this and that she wouldn't usually let anything get in the way of chasing down a goal. But she has let me know that she won't be out running with me in the morning and is obviously prioritising her evening with Ryan over the upcoming marathon.

What a weak mindset.

I type out a reply to Lucy to let her know that it's not a problem and that I hope she is feeling better soon, even though I know it's all nonsense because there's absolutely nothing wrong with her. But I obviously don't want her to know how I know that, so I've been discreet and played it safe.

But Lucy doesn't text me back to say thanks for being understanding or offering me best wishes. She just goes back to eating her dessert and chatting away with Ryan.

It's a few minutes later when I notice them finish their meal, which is pleasing and not just because I'm freezing cold out here waiting for them to leave. It's also because I've been treated to several amazing aromas wafting out of that restaurant whenever the front door has opened or closed, and I am absolutely starving now. But there will be time to eat later.

I'm really hoping the pair in the restaurant don't order another round of drinks because that will only prolong my stay out here, so I'm very pleased to see the waiter bring over the bill a few minutes later. From my vantage point, it looks like Ryan has picked up the tab, which is very gentlemanly of him. I wonder if he knows how much Lucy made this week with her bonus. If he did, he might not be in so much of a rush to get his debit card out.

The pair stand up from the table a moment later and put their coats on before they head for the door, chatting and laughing as they go. I guess the date has gone well. The only question now is:

Is it over?

I get my answer when I see the pair of them stick together as they walk away down the street. They haven't parted yet, and as I follow them at a safe distance, it doesn't look like they will. They are going somewhere new together. But where?

It's a funny combination of nerves and excitement that I'm feeling as I follow Lucy and Ryan because I've never done this kind of thing before, and I certainly don't want to get caught doing it. But there's a certain power in watching someone who doesn't know they are being watched, and it feels good to have something over Lucy, even if she isn't aware of it yet.

The pair eventually stop outside several flats, and I wonder whose home they are about to go in now. I get my answer when I see Lucy use her electronic key fob to open the gate, and as the pair shuffle inside, I wonder how long they are going to be in there for. All night? That would be a problem for me because I don't want to wait that long for what I want.

I let out a frustrated sigh before sitting down on the edge of a garden wall and killing some time by playing some Sudoku on my phone. I got into this game after competing against another user on the app in which we were both given a series of puzzles to solve, and the winner was the one who solved them first. It was good fun, particularly when I won, and I have played the game ever since.

I wonder if I would have carried on with it if I had lost that contest. Probably not because Sudoku would have been ruined for me then. I detest anything that I associate with loss and failure, and that's why I hate Lucy so much. All I see when I look at her is my own shortcomings reflected back. But not for much longer. Soon, she will be the one who looks at me and feels worthless, and I very much look forward to that day.

I've managed to complete six Sudoku puzzles in around half an hour, and I'm just about considering giving up and going home when I hear the gate opening outside Lucy's flat again. When I look up, I see Ryan walking out.

That's a surprise. I guess he isn't staying overnight after all.

And he doesn't look too happy about it either.

He has his hands stuffed into his coat pockets and his shoulders slouched as he shuffles away down the street, and I wonder what happened.

But that's not all I do.

I start following him too.

28

LUCY

'Do you think I did the right thing?'

I'm asking Kirsty for advice whilst being consumed by doubt after what I did last night. I asked Ryan to leave, not because I didn't want him to stay but because I didn't want to rush things between us. We kissed in my bedroom but didn't go any further than that, not that Ryan wasn't keen to. But I put the brakes on and explained to him that I really liked him, and because of that, I didn't want things to go too fast.

He seemed to understand, although he was perhaps understandably a little frustrated having been invited into my room, but he left on good terms, and we agreed that we would see each other again very soon. But having been comfortable with my decision last night as I drifted off to sleep, I have woken up this morning full of doubt about whether or not I did the right thing or if I've just blown my chances with the first guy I've been interested in for a long time. That's why I'm asking my flatmate for her opinion on the matter. She has more experience with this kind of thing, after all.

'Hmmm, it's a difficult one,' she admits as she hands me a cup of tea and takes a seat at the kitchen table with me. 'On one hand, I can see what you were thinking. But on the other, I can see why Ryan might have felt like you were having doubts.'

'But I'm not having doubts. I'm sure things are going great. That's why I did it. Because this feels real rather than just some casual thing.'

I notice then that Kirsty is grinning widely at me, and I have to ask her why that is.

'I've never seen you like this,' she tells me, still grinning, which I take to mean she is enjoying seeing this side of me.

'What? I'm still the same,' I try, but my flatmate isn't buying it.

'Are you joking? You're usually up and out the door at the crack of dawn for exercise or trying to do something for some challenge that you're competing in on your phone. Yet here you are, sitting in your pyjamas at midday, asking me for relationship advice.'

'That's not what I'm doing!'

'Isn't it?'

'No, I'm just making conversation!'

'Oh, right. I see. It's funny how you've never made conversation about a guy before, but now all I hear is Ryan this and Ryan that.'

Kirsty is clearly amused by all of this, and I'm happy that she is happy, but she's not been much help so far.

'Look, all I want to know is, did I mess things up last night by asking him to leave?'

'No, I don't think so,' Kirsty says quite confidently, which sets my mind at ease a little. 'If he respects you, which I'm sure he does, then he won't have had a problem with it.'

'Cool. That's what I was hoping you'd say.'

'Of course, he might have needed to take a cold shower when he got home.'

'Kirsty!'

I laugh at my friend's inappropriate joke before we move on.

'So, have you heard from lover boy today?'

'Yeah, he texted me this morning. Said he's going over to his parents for Sunday lunch.'

'Awww, a family man. How sweet. He sounds like a keeper. Should I start helping you prepare the wedding invites?'

'Ha, you wish.'

'I do wish. I really want to be a bridesmaid.'

'Yeah, well you'll have a long wait if you're waiting for me to walk down that aisle.'

'Maybe not that long if you keep swooning over Ryan.'

I roll my eyes and decide that I've had enough of talking about my love life with my best friend, so I change the subject quickly.

'What have you got planned today?' I ask Kirsty as I finish my tea.

'Not much. Maybe a bit of shopping. Want to join me?'

'Hmmm, I don't know. I really should go for a run.'

'I thought you cancelled on Jess?'

'Yeah, I did. But that was before I changed my mind about having Ryan stay over for the night. I should probably have gone and met her, really.'

'I'm sure she didn't mind.'

172

'Yeah, I hope not.'

'What's the deal with her, anyway? You used to talk about her a lot, but now you barely mention her.'

I'm surprised that Kirsty has picked up on how things have changed a little between Jess and I, but she obviously has if she's bringing it up.

'I'm not sure. I mean, we're still friends and everything, but I'm not sure if me getting a job at the same place as her has changed things between us.'

'In what way?'

'I don't know. It's just we're in the same team, and with it being sales, it's already a competitive environment before you even factor in both our personalities. I'm not sure that's conducive to us being mates.'

'Has she said anything to you?'

'No, she's still being nice.'

'Maybe everything's okay then.'

'Yeah, maybe. It's just I worry that she might be a little jealous.'

'Jealous. How?'

'Because I've come in and won the first bonus.'

'If she's jealous of your success then she isn't really a friend, is she?'

'I suppose not. Maybe it's not jealousy then. Resentment, perhaps.'

'That sounds even worse!'

'I don't know then. I'm probably just being paranoid.'

'You could just ask her.'

'Ask her what? If she hates me?'

'No, be a little more subtle than that.'

I think about it for a moment but decide to leave it.

'I'm sure it's fine,' I say. 'We'll either be friends or we won't. If not, then I guess I've got you, haven't I?'

'And aren't you lucky!'

We laugh again before Kirsty tells me she wants to get into town before the shops close earlier on this Sunday. But I decide that I'm not going to go with her. Instead, I go and change into my running gear and perform a couple of stretches before heading out the door for another run. I'm still feeling a little jaded after indulging in all those glasses of wine last night, but I soon blow off the cobwebs, and I'm feeling much better once I get into a good stride and feel the wind blowing in my face.

Running really is a great way to change a mood and get a natural high, and the longer I run for, the less I feel stressed about whether I upset Ryan last night. I simply made an adult decision with him, and he took it like an adult, so there's nothing to fear there.

I also feel less worried about Jess and whether or not she likes me less than when we first met as I keep jogging and releasing those endorphins. I'm sure everything is fine there too because it usually is in the end.

If only I'd known then how wrong I was about that then I wouldn't have been feeling quite so good. Instead, I'd have been worried.

For me.

And for Ryan.

29

JESS

Sunday. A great day for a drive.

Some people like to make their way into town for a bit of shopping and a roast dinner. Others like to take their vehicle out into the countryside and really pick up some speed before returning to more populated areas for another busy week ahead.

So, where have I chosen to drive to today?

Simple. *I'm going wherever the car in front of me is going.*

I've been following Ryan's car ever since I watched him leave his place and get in behind the wheel five minutes ago, having returned to his address this morning with my car once I knew where he lived. With that knowledge, I was able to get on his tail, and as we come to a stop at a set of traffic lights, I can see his eyes in his windscreen mirror up ahead.

But he won't be aware that anything is out of the ordinary. To him, I'm just another car on the road driving behind him, sure to turn off at some point because I'll have a different destination to him. Except I don't. I am going to stay behind him, although not long enough for him to get suspicious.

I'll make my move before that happens.

The lights turn green, and we're on the move again, moving through town, although not for long. Ryan indicates left, so I follow suit, and the pair of us transition onto the next road. It's quieter here, and it appears that Ryan is heading away from the busier part of town and into the more suburban areas. That means I can't follow him for too much longer.

It's time to act now.

I increase my speed and close the distance between our cars a little as he approaches the next junction. But while he taps the brakes and I see the red lights go on in the rear of his car that should warn me to brake too, I do the opposite.

I speed up.

And then I feel the inevitable collision.

It's louder than I thought it would be, and a little more violent, but I wasn't going fast enough to do either of us any serious damage. It was just enough to bump into Ryan's car and let him know it happened.

But now that it has, I'm guessing he won't be too happy about it.

I see his hazard lights go on before the driver's door opens, and he gets out, looking back to see who has just been stupid enough to drive into the back of him. I follow suit with the hazard lights before getting out of my own car and as soon as I do, I am full of apologies.

'Oh my gosh, I'm so sorry!' I cry as I see Ryan rushing around to survey the damage.

'What happened?' he wants to know, looking from my car to his own and not understanding how they have come to be stuck together.

'I don't know. I think my foot slipped off the brake pedal,' I say. 'It's all my fault. I'm so sorry.'

Ryan still looks tense, but I think the fact that I am so openly admitting fault here is at least consoling him that I won't cause any problems with paying to sort this mess out.

'Are you insured?' he asks me.

'Yeah. You?'

'Yep.'

'Good. Well, don't worry, I'll sort all of this out. It was my fault, and I'll pay to get it fixed.'

'Erm, yeah. Okay,' Ryan says as he runs a hand through his hair while staring at the damaged paintwork. 'I guess we should exchange details then.'

He takes out his phone and I do the same as some of the traffic behind us starts manoeuvring around.

'What's your name?' Ryan asks after I have given him my number.

'Milly,' I reply without skipping a beat.

'I'm Ryan,' he tells me as I save his number, and I nod my head like I had no idea what he was called until he just told me.

'We better get a couple of photos, just in case we need them later,' Ryan says after that, and I wonder if he's just doing that because he doesn't quite trust me to do the right thing and sort this out through my insurance company once we have driven off. But I don't mind that, and so I agree with him, stepping back so he can take a few pictures without me in them.

'So, you'll be in touch when you've spoken to your insurers?' he asks me as he puts his phone away.

'Yeah, definitely. I'll call them when I get home, and I'll keep you updated.'

'Okay, cool.'

'Look, I'm really sorry again for this. I don't know how I managed it.'

'It's okay. Accidents happen. Let's just get it sorted out quickly so we can get our cars fixed. Will you be okay to drive?'

It's sweet that he's asking about my wellbeing, considering I've just put a big dent in the back of his vehicle, and I can see why Lucy likes this guy. He really is a gentleman, even in difficult times.

'Yeah, I'll be fine. Don't worry about me,' I tell him with a smile, and I make sure to hold his gaze until he breaks it, hinting that I'm not just some ditzy woman who can't drive properly but a fun, flirtatious one too.

'Okay, well I guess we'll speak soon,' he says, showing me the briefest of smiles before he gets back into his car.

I get back behind the wheel of my own vehicle and wait for him to drive away before I do the same, but I'm not following him anymore, so I can head in a different direction.

As our cars separate, I keep the smile on my face as I shift gears and drive my partially damaged vehicle home. Yes, maybe I'm going to have to pay some repair costs on my car at some point to make it officially roadworthy again, but if I do, that's a small price to pay for what I have just been able to get.

Ryan's phone number.

Now I have that, I can do anything.

I keep grinning all the way home as I think about what I am going to do with the newly acquired contact details. Not only do I have a way of getting in touch with Ryan without having to follow him anymore, I also have a very valid reason to be messaging him, and he will be eager to hear from me. Granted, he'll only want to hear from me because he'll want confirmation that my insurance will cover the cost of his repairs, but once we are communicating, he'll learn that this doesn't just have to be some simple transactional relationship.

He's going to get a surprise when I do start texting him.

But I think he's going to like it.

30

LUCY

I was enjoying a lazy Sunday evening with Kirsty watching some cookery show on the TV when I noticed that Ryan was calling me. I was surprised to see his name flash up on my phone in this way because we'd only ever texted before, but I answered quickly and hoped he wasn't ringing me to say that he was ending things after what happened last night.

'Hey, how was Sunday lunch at your parents' place?' I ask him, hoping to start the conversation off on a light note.

'It was great, but you'll never guess what happened to me on the way over there.'

'What?'

'Someone drove into the back of my car.'

'What? Are you okay?'

My loud cries see Kirsty look at me with a confused expression on her face as she tries to figure out what's going on, but I ignore her until I hear what happened from Ryan.

'Yeah, I'm fine,' he tells me, and I let out a sigh of relief before giving Kirsty a thumbs-up so she can go back to watching the TV without worry.

'So, what happened?'

'Some woman just drove right into the back of me. She said her foot slipped off the brake.'

'What an idiot.'

181

'It was an accident.'

'Was she okay?'

'Yeah, she's fine, and she's accepted the blame for it.'

'That's good. It shouldn't cost you anything then.'

'Yeah, just the hassle of dealing with insurers, but it could be worse, I suppose.'

'Well, I'm glad you're okay,' I say, and I notice Kirsty look at me again, and this time, she is making a face that tells me she thinks it's cute that I'm so concerned about him.

I decide to conduct the rest of this phone call in a different room so it's not distracting, so I get up off the sofa, leaving Kirsty and her silly facial expressions behind.

'So, is everything else okay?' I ask Ryan once I am in my room with the door closed behind me.

'Yeah, it's fine.'

'Oh, good. I was a little worried.'

'Why?'

'I don't know. Just with what happened last night.'

'It was fine. I told you.'

'I know, but I can see how it was a little misleading by me to bring you back to my place and then ask you to leave.'

'Don't worry about it, honestly.'

'So we're good?'

'Of course we are.'

I smile at that confirmation, and it's also proof that I was worrying unnecessarily earlier before I went on my run and put myself into a better frame of mind.

We chat for several more minutes, and I tell him all about what I have been up to, although it's a lot less dramatic than his story. Then we end the call but not before he has invited me over to his place in a couple of days for a takeaway after work.

As I leave my room and return to my place on the sofa beside Kirsty, I wonder if he has invited me to his so there can't be a repeat of me throwing him out if he came here. But he's probably just returning the favour in letting me see his place after I showed him mine. I'm excited to see where he lives, and I'm just hoping that there isn't anything there to concern me and put an end to this blossoming romance, like finding out he is a hoarder or that he has a sink full of dirty dishes dating back months.

Kirsty turns the volume down on the TV as I tell her about the 'car crash' Ryan was in, and she is just as shocked as I was but also pleased that he came out of it unscathed. Then it doesn't take her long to start teasing me again.

'Your voice got very high-pitched when you asked him if he was okay,' Kirsty says with a smile. 'You were very concerned.'

'Of course I was concerned! He could have been seriously hurt!'

'That would have been unfortunate after it's taken you so long to find a boyfriend.'

'He's not my boyfriend!'

'Not officially, but it seems like it's just a matter of time now.'

'Shut up, and let's watch TV,' I say to my friend as I grab the remote and turn the volume back up.

I shake my head as Kirsty chuckles at me, but as I sit there watching the TV, I think about whether I should let Ryan know that I'm interested in making things official between us the next time I see him. He clearly likes me as much as I like him, and while I had no intention of getting in a relationship any time soon, I guess life has a habit of being unpredictable.

I think about what being someone's girlfriend could mean for everything else I do. It will mean I will have less free time for one thing because I'll have to spend time with Ryan and presumably meet his family and friends at some point. That will mean I won't have as much time to keep up some of my hobbies, although there are some things I'll never stop, like running, because I love to do that for my mental wellbeing. But maybe it's not a bad thing if I cut something out, and if I had to choose something, I'd guess it would be the app where I compete against strangers.

I used to live for that app and the competition it provided me, but I've barely used it over these last few weeks, and I'm not sure I actually need to start doing so again. I could just get my fix of competition in my new job, and based on how things have started there, I reckon I will get more than enough of that with the likes of Jess around.

That's decided it. I'll do the thing that Kirsty wanted me to do a long time ago and delete the app so I can have a more well-rounded and balanced life. No more getting up at the crack of dawn to try and outperform some randomer on the internet, or cancelling social events because the time is running out on a challenge and I need to make sure I win it. I'll never lose that competitive streak that I have within me, but meeting Ryan and seeing what I have been missing out on all these years has caused me to reconsider the way I was living, and that is probably a good thing.

With the app no longer on my phone, I feel strangely unburdened, but I'm glad I didn't do this a few weeks ago. If I had then I would never have met Jess, and I wouldn't have ended up working at the same place as her and making all this extra money. Timing is everything, and life has a habit of making things work out for the best in the end.

Or so I thought.

31

JESS

It's been a couple of days since I deliberately drove my car into Ryan's, and I've been biding my time ever since then so that what I do next seems more plausible. I sent him a message yesterday to say that I had contacted my insurer and they would get back to me shortly with more information about how to proceed, but in reality, I've done no such thing. I haven't let my insurer know about the 'accident' because I'm not planning on being the one to pay for it all. Ryan will.

I just need to warm him up to the idea of it.

It's been another long day in the office, but I wasn't in the mood for trying to outlast Lucy and stay at my desk longer than her tonight. I just wanted to go home because I've got bigger fish to fry than that. But I noticed that she was leaving at a decent time too, and she had mentioned something about going to Ryan's place this evening.

That should be cosy.

But it's time for me to interrupt whatever fun they are having.

I'm lying on my bed with my phone in my hand and a mischievous grin on my face. That's because I'm about to let Ryan know that there's a slight problem and that we're going to have to meet to discuss it.

In private.

I wonder what he might be up to right now with Lucy as I compose my message. Are they eating dinner together? Watching TV? Or has he already shown her the bedroom? That last one is doubtful based on the fact I not only saw him leaving Lucy's apartment when he might have expected to stay the night, but Lucy has mentioned to me in the office that she is taking things slowly with her new man when I asked about her love life in passing the other day.

But whatever those two lovebirds are doing, I'm about to get in the way of it.

'Hi Ryan. It's Milly. How's it going? Just wanted to let you know that my insurance company have come back to me and there's a slight problem. But nothing I can't sort out so don't worry! I hope you're having a good evening x'

The kiss at the end is a bold move, but I bet that won't even be the thing that he pays most attention to. That will be the part where I mentioned there was a problem because even though I have made sure to keep things seem light, he will want to know what I am referring to.

Sure enough, it doesn't take him long to respond to my text with one of his own.

'Hi Milly. Thanks for the update. What's the problem?'

There's no kiss at the end of his message, but that won't slow me down because I've achieved what I wanted to.

I've got his attention.

'It's just that I think it's going to cost me a lot more than I anticipated. I guess I'm going to have to cut back on all my girly nights out! But not to worry. I'll figure it out somehow. It was my fault. I'm such an idiot! x'

I wait for him to reply to my latest message, hoping he will fall into the trap I am laying for him. Sure enough, he does.

'You're not an idiot. It was just an accident. How much are they quoting?'

Still no kiss. But he's being nice to me.

'You wouldn't believe it if I told you! But don't worry, I'll figure it out. I'll sell a kidney if I have to! Ha! x'

I'm laying it on a little thick, but I want him to think that I have a bit of a problem now that I'm struggling to solve. That way we can get to the part where I give him a solution.

'Don't be silly! It can't be that much, can it? x'

Yes! I've done it. I've got him to copy me and put a kiss at the end of his text. It's only a small thing, but it's proof that we can start moving beyond just being two strangers whose cars collided. Now that I have that promising sign, it's time to switch gears.

'Would it be possible for us to meet somewhere quickly this week? It'll be easier to explain in person rather than over the phone xx'

Two kisses now. Let's see how he likes that.

But he doesn't respond for almost ten minutes, and I'm starting to worry that I've messed things up. Did

I go too fast? Should I have slowplayed things a little more? Am I going to have to come up with another plan?

Then he texts me back, and I exhale.

'Sure. Do you work in town? We could meet at lunchtime tomorrow if so x'

He's stayed steady at one kiss, but that's fine. The important thing is that he is willing to meet me.

'Yeah, I can tomorrow! Perfect! How about Miller's at midday? xx'

Miller's is a cool little Irish pub that serves great food at all hours of the day but especially at lunchtimes, and while it's not the kind of place I hang out in too often, I'm betting Ryan won't say no to a trip there.

'Okay, sure. I'll see you then x'

'Awesome! Thank you! See you tomorrow :) xx'

Capping it off with a smiley face just seemed right to me, and it's made sure to end this text conversation on a positive note. I've accomplished what I needed to, and now I will be meeting with Ryan tomorrow. Perfect. I look forward to leaving my desk at lunchtime and leaving Lucy to work hard at hers while I go out for lunch to meet her man.

She'll have no idea what I'm up to, even if Ryan is to mention that the woman who hit his car wants to meet him to discuss. But I doubt he will. Why would he tell her and risk Lucy wanting to see the messages? Then she would see all the kisses, particularly the ones he sent to me, and she might get jealous. No guy would want to start some drama, so I bet he won't say a word to her about it. Even if he does, the fake name I've been working under won't alert Lucy. I've covered every angle.

Putting my phone down after a satisfactory night's work, I spend the rest of the evening watching videos on my laptop in which endurance runners share their best tips for achieving peak performance in a marathon. That upcoming event is still very much on my mind, whether or not Lucy is alongside me at the start line on the big day. Her participation remains to be seen because after what I am going to do to her, she might not feel like racing me.

If all goes well, she'll want to kill me.

32

LUCY

I've been fighting the urge to ask Ryan who he has been messaging tonight ever since I noticed his phone screen flashing with notifications and his fingers typing out several texts. But I'm aware that a question like that could make me come across as a little paranoid, so that's why I've not said anything yet. We're not officially in a relationship, so why should I care who he is messaging and what he might be saying in those messages? We're just two unattached people hanging out together.

But maybe it's time to change that.

I'm sitting in Ryan's flat beside him on the sofa in front of his impressive flatscreen TV on which we are watching a movie that he clearly put on just to impress me. It's one that's full of actors and actresses that are only known for playing romantic parts, and there's no way he would have chosen this if I wasn't here. I know that for sure because I can see his DVD collection on the shelf behind the TV, and it's full of Schwarzenegger movies from the 80's and 90's. That's another strong sign that this guy really likes me, to go with all the other signs like the lovely meal he just cooked for me and the fact he has invited me over here in the first place.

I wait until he has finished writing his latest text and put his phone down again before I take the plunge.

'I think things are going really well, don't you?' I say, starting gently.

'Huh?' Ryan mumbles, and I think he has presumed I'm referring to something in the film that he hasn't been paying attention to.

'With us. Things are going well, right?'

'Oh, yeah. I think so.'

I smile, but I know that the next part will be harder to say. God, I'm useless at this. I really should have spent more time working on this aspect of my life because maybe I wouldn't feel so awkward now.

'Do you think we should….' I start but drift off, unsure how to finish that sentence.

'What?'

This is not going as well as I thought. Maybe I can make actions speak louder than words.

'You know, there's one room you haven't shown me yet,' I say with a wry grin, and while it takes a little longer than it should for Ryan to get which room I am referring to, he almost leaps out of his seat when he does.

'Oh, right! Okay!' he says before I lean in for a kiss.

When our lips finally part, it doesn't take us long to take things into the bedroom, and now that I've decided that I'm done with going slow, things get fast real quick.

I don't know how long the whole thing lasted, but it was certainly well worth the wait, and as the pair of us lie beside each other under the bedsheets, breathless and beaming, it's clear our relationship has just moved into the next phase. But just to make sure, I check with Ryan.

'So, are we official now or what?' I ask him with a laugh.

'I think we are,' he replies before rolling over and giving me another kiss.

It feels good to have his arms wrapped around me, and for the first time in a long time, I don't feel anxious or like I have to get up and do something to try and impress somebody. Just lying here in his arms is fine with me. It's safe, comforting, and it's less stressful than always trying to be the best version of myself at all times. Of course, I'll still always try and represent myself in the best manner out in public in front of other people like Jess, for example, but here with Ryan, I can relax and not worry about things like that. He's not a competitor, he's my lover, and now he is officially my boyfriend.

I laugh out loud at that moment when I think of something, and Ryan wants to know what's so funny.

'I was just thinking about how Kirsty will react when I tell her,' I say. 'You have no idea how long she has been wanting me to get a boyfriend.'

'I take it there will be some double dates for us to go on now then?'

'Yeah, I imagine there will be. That okay?'

'Sure. Any excuse for a night out.'

We kiss again, and I feel like I could stay like this all night. Maybe I could.

'Do you want me to stay over?' I ask Ryan, and he doesn't seem to have a problem with that at all.

'I might get a snack from the fridge. Do you want anything?' he asks me as he continues to kiss my cheek.

'Nah, I'm good, thanks. I haven't worked up an appetite just yet.'

I give him a wink, and he laughs as he peels back the duvet and scampers out of the room in just his boxer shorts while I stay in the warm bed and wait for him to return. But it's as I am lying there that I hear the vibration from his mobile phone on the bedside table, and when I look over at it, I see he has just received a new message.

It's from someone called Milly, and she is asking Ryan if they can meet at 12:30 instead of 12 because she has just remembered she has a meeting in the morning that might overrun.

I presume this is something to do with work, but I decide to check anyway when Ryan walks back into the bedroom chomping on a slice of ham he must have found in the fridge.

'I just heard your phone,' I say to him as I gesture towards his device on the table. 'I think you've got a message.'

'Oh, cool,' he says as he walks over to check on it, and I watch him reading it while he continues chewing before my curiosity gets the better of me.

'Who's Milly?'

'Huh?'

'Sorry, I noticed her name when I heard the message.'

'Oh, right. It's the woman who hit my car.'

That wasn't what I was expecting to hear.

'Why is she messaging you?' I ask.

'She's trying to sort it all out with her insurers.'

'And has she?'

'Not yet. But I'm sure she will.'

'Why does she want to meet you?'

'What?'

'The message said she wants to meet.'

Maybe I am in danger of coming across as a little overbearing in these early stages, but I want to know.

'Oh, yeah. Erm, she said there was a problem, and she needed to talk to me.'

'Couldn't she just ring you?'

'I don't know. I guess.'

'Do you think she's trying to get out of paying for the accident?'

'I doubt it. She's admitted fault, and I have the evidence.'

'So I wonder why she wants to meet you.'

'I don't know. I'll let you know when I do.'

That seems fair enough, so I leave it at that, not wanting to spoil this great evening we have been having by prying too much into this bad driver who wants to meet Ryan. I'm sure it is just something to do with the insurers. Maybe she wants him to sign some paperwork or something.

Who knows?

I guess he'll tell me tomorrow.

33

JESS

I'm glad I altered the time that I had arranged to meet Ryan because, as I suspected, my morning meeting did overrun a little. But I'm still on track to make it to Miller's for 12:30, and I'm very much looking forward to this as I make my way through reception and out of the office.

I didn't have to worry about Lucy asking me where I was going for lunch because she was still busy in a meeting with Greg when it came time for me to put my coat on and leave. While it irritates me that she is clearly still in our boss's inner circle and being privy to whatever plans he has for the company next, I know that won't seem like much consolation to Lucy when all of this plays out and the dust settles.

She might have won a few battles, but I will win the war.

It doesn't take me long to make it to Miller's, and I enter through the front door behind a couple of giggling Irish men in cheap suits who are clearly excited about the prospect of a lunchtime pint or two. Once I'm in, I spot Ryan seated at one of the tables by the window, chatting to a barmaid in a black shirt with the pub's logo on the front of it.

Ryan spots me walking over, and as I reach the table, it seems as though there is a bit of uncertainty as to whether or not we are staying here for long. He hasn't taken a menu from the barmaid, nor has he placed an order for a drink, so he's obviously wondering if this meeting will be a quick one. But I remove all uncertainty by asking for a glass of white wine and accepting a menu from the barmaid with a smile.

I tell Ryan that we might as well get lunch while we're here, and he reluctantly agrees, ordering himself a beer and taking his own menu before we settle in while the barmaid rushes away to fetch our drinks.

'Thanks for coming,' I say once she is out of earshot. 'Sorry if it's a bit of a hassle for you.'

'No, it's okay,' Ryan assures me. 'So, is everything okay with the insurers?'

He's getting straight down to business, but that's okay. The sooner we get that over with, the sooner we can talk about something more interesting.

'Kind of,' I begin, nibbling my bottom lip to make myself seem nervous.

'What is it?'

'It's the price they have given me to get all of this fixed. It's higher than I thought it would be.'

'How much?'

'They're saying almost a thousand pounds, and that's just to fix my car. I don't even know what yours will cost yet.'

'How much? That's ridiculous!'

'I know. But that's what they told me.'

'I'll get someone to look at it myself.'

'No, I don't want you to go to any trouble. This was my fault.'

'It's fine. We just need to sort it out as quickly as possible so we aren't driving around with dents in our cars.'

The barmaid returns then with our drinks, and we thank her before taking a sip.

'I would say cheers, but I'm not sure it's the right occasion for it,' I jest, and Ryan laughs.

'You know, you could have just told me this over the phone,' he tells me.

'I suppose, but then…' I let my sentence trail off before saying 'never mind.'

'What?' Ryan asks, curious as to what it was that I was going to say.

'No, it's silly. Forget about it,' I tell him, but I know full well he won't leave it there.

'Tell me,' he pleads, and I grimace as I pretend like I have been forced into this.

'Well, it's just that, I might have been looking for an excuse to see you again,' I say with a nervous smile.

'Why?'

'Why do you think?'

'Oh, erm, okay,' Ryan mumbles, clearly caught off guard now that he has figured it out.

'But it was wrong of me to do that. You're right. I could have just told you over the phone and saved us having to come here on our lunch break.'

'No, it's okay. It's just a surprise, that's all.'

'A good one or a bad one?' I ask with a mischievous grin, but Ryan still looks uncomfortable, and it's clear he's not ready for full-on flirting just yet.

'Erm, I don't know,' he mumbles before picking up his drink and taking a thirsty gulp.

'I'm sorry if I've made you feel awkward,' I say. 'I should just pay the costs and get it over with. It's just…'

'What?'

'I'm struggling for money at the moment.'

That couldn't be further from the truth, but I hope Ryan believes it, and to aid my cause, I made sure to wear my cheapest work attire to the office today.

'Oh, I see.'

'But this is my problem, and I'll find a way to fix it. Unless…'

'Unless what?'

'We could come to an arrangement.'

I let the words hang in the air between us, and the tension is only cut by the barmaid returning to take our food order.

I deliberately wait for Ryan to speak first because I want to know what he plans to do after what I've just said to him. Is he going to run out of this bar and get away from me? Or is he going to stay and continue our discussion?'

'I'll have the burger, please,' he says, and that gives me my answer.

He's not going anywhere.

'Just the chicken salad for me, please,' I say as I hand my menu back to the barmaid, and as she leaves us again, I notice Ryan taking another long gulp of his drink.

I let another heavy moment of silence pass between us again before I speak, and this time, it's to ask him what he thinks of my proposal.

'What kind of arrangement?' he wants to know, and I roll my eyes before leaning in a little closer across the table and holding his gaze.

'You seem like a smart guy. I'm sure you can figure it out.'

The look that flashes across his face lets me know that he has figured out now if he hadn't done so already, and I nod my head to reinforce the idea.

'Perhaps if you help me out with the cost of the repairs for the cars, I could help you out with something,' I go on teasingly. 'Anything you can think of. Just say the word.'

Ryan has looked a little awkward almost the whole time we have been sitting here, but now he seems to be relaxing a little. I guess it feels good for a man to hear that a woman is willing to do anything he wants for him.

'Unless, of course, you're married or have a girlfriend,' I say, pretending to be thoughtful. 'But I didn't see a wedding ring on your hand the other day, and I'm hoping you're single.'

Ryan pauses before answering, and I wonder if he will dare mention Lucy and how he is supposed to be seeing her and no one else.

'Erm, no. I'm not married,' he mumbles. 'And I've not got a girlfriend.'

'Interesting,' I say as I take a sip of my wine while maintaining eye contact with him. 'That would have been a real shame.'

'So, what are you suggesting?' Ryan asks as he tries to contain his excitement.

'How about you come to my place this evening and find out?' I tell him, and that is all it takes to seal the deal.

We spend the rest of lunchtime talking about what we do for work as we eat our lunch, but I'm so comfortable at lying that I have no trouble reeling off some lies about how I work in office administration while I chomp on my salad. By the time we finish and leave the table, Ryan has offered to pay, and I tell him that I'm finding him sexier by the minute.

Once outside the pub, we say our goodbyes because we need to get back to our respective workplaces, but before we part, I give Ryan my address and tell him to text me when he is on his way around this evening.

'Give me a little warning,' I advise him. 'So I can make sure I'm really ready for you.'

I wonder how long it will take for the grin to come off Ryan's face as he turns and walks back to his office, but it's probably just as long as it will take for the one on my face to fade too. I can't help smiling now, and why shouldn't I?

I've just secured a hot date with Lucy's man, and unsurprisingly, I no longer feel like the loser between the pair of us.

34

LUCY

I'm not sure what game Jess is playing these days, but she certainly doesn't seem as competitive in the workplace as she was when I first started working with her. Instead of trying to stay at her desk later than me, this is the second night in a row she has finished up before me and wished me a good night. Either she is on top of all of her work, or she has plans this evening that are more important than anything she has to do here. Whatever the case, she is out the door before me again, and I'm left to finish up my work without her to keep me company.

But she was in a very cheery mood this afternoon as she asked me how my training for the marathon was going, before saying that we must get another run in together soon. She joked about how she needed a new pair of running trainers because she was wearing the insoles out of her current pair, as well as telling me that she was turning into one of those sad runners who become so obsessed with the sport that they spend their free time trawling through online forums reading what other runners have to say.

I told her that my training wasn't quite as intensive as this, although that was more down to the fact that I have been busy with my new partner rather than any laziness to put my trainers on and go for a run. But hearing that Jess is taking the marathon seriously has reminded me that I need to do the same, otherwise I'll be in danger of getting shown up, not that it would be the end of the world if I did.

Ryan has really changed my perspective on things, and these days, losing at one or two things doesn't seem as unbearable as it once did. It's funny, but I wonder if Ryan will ever get to know the old me now that I'm not like that as much. I suppose he will only know how competitive I used to be if I tell him, but I'm not sure I want to. He might find it unappealing, just like Kirsty used to do. I think I'll leave that part of myself hidden away and only bring it out when I need it.

With the office emptying out, I decide that it's time for me to call it a day too, so I log off and leave my desk, saying a cheery 'goodnight' to the security guard on the way out. Then, as I make my way home, I decide to call Ryan and see what he is up to this evening.

We don't have any plans to meet tonight, but I've been so busy all day that I have failed to respond to his last text message asking me how things were going, so I'll call and let him know that I'm still alive. When he answers, I can tell that he is driving because I can hear a lot of noise in the background, so I assume he is talking to me on his hands-free set.

'Hey! How's it going?' I say as I cross a street with several other commuters.

'Yeah, good thanks. Busy day?'

'Always! You?'

'Same.'

'So, what are you up to?'

'I'm just driving to the gym.'

'Good for you.'

'Yeah. Then I'll probably just grab some food from somewhere and have an early night.'

'Sounds nice.'

'What about you?'

'I need to go for a run. But other than that, I've not got much else on.'

I'm almost hoping here that Ryan might invite me around to his to spend the night once he has done everything he needs to do, but he doesn't do that. I suppose I can't be too upset about that. I did spend last night at his, and these are still early days for us. It's just having spent so many years sleeping alone, I rather enjoyed waking up beside him this morning.

'Well, I better go. I'm almost at the gym. Have a good run.'

'Thanks. Enjoy your workout. Text me later, yeah?'

'Will do. Bye!'

Ryan hangs up, and I feel content as I put my phone back in my handbag and carry on walking home. While it would have been good to see him, I like the fact that he is busy and has plenty of other things to keep him occupied when he's not with me. And I don't think any woman should complain if their man is willing to go to the gym and keep fit of their own accord.

I almost feel like I want to run a little extra now this evening once I have my trainers on because I know that Ryan is going to be working up a sweat. And I suppose now I have another reason to keep fit. It's not just to be better in my athletic performance, it's to look better when I'm in the bedroom with my man.

The flat is empty when I get home, as I expected it would be because Kirsty told me she was going out for a few drinks with her work pals tonight. That's why I put a little music on as I get changed for my run, singing my heart out to a couple of ballads that I would almost certainly be too embarrassed to sing to if someone else was around to hear me.

It's been a while since I gave my vocal chords a stretch, and it usually only happens when I'm drunk and find myself in some bar or pub that offers Karaoke, but the fact I'm singing so loud and proud now tells me that I'm feeling happy. I guess I've got a lot to be happy about. I've got a great job, a best friend and a wonderful new man.

All is certainly well in my world.

And long may it continue.

35

JESS

The water is warm and soothing on my skin as I stand beneath the shower head and smile to myself. My eyes are closed, but not because I'm trying to protect them from any soapy suds that might run into them and cause them to sting. They're closed because that's the easiest way for me to re-imagine what I've just finished doing.

Ryan's topless torso.

The weight of him on top of me.

And the feeling when he kissed my lips.

As I made it clear to Lucy's boyfriend earlier during our lunchtime meeting, he had a fun time waiting in store for him if he was to call by my place this evening.

And call by he did.

I answered the door to him wearing a silky black dressing gown that I knew he would like, along with a suggestive smile that he was quick to reciprocate before he came in and I offered him a drink. I was glad that he had turned up, but I had been afraid that he might have been a little shy or nervous considering he was here without the knowledge of his girlfriend, who would have quite rightly wanted to kill him if she had found out where he was.

But Ryan hadn't been nervous. He had been quite bold and had stopped me just as I was pouring him a drink and kissed me with a passion and determination

x

208

that suggested he was someone who wanted to do this kind of thing more often but didn't get the chance. I guess Lucy isn't keeping him as happy as she presumably thinks she is.

There was no need for any mention of insurance companies or repair costs after that as we made our way quickly into the bedroom, where we spent the next hour under the sheets. Having started this whole thing simply as a way of getting back at Lucy, I hadn't gone into it expecting to particularly enjoy the intimate part of the process, but Ryan was a surprisingly affectionate lover, and I had fun during the time we were together.

If the guilt did come on his side, it came once we had finished and he was putting his clothes back on. That was when he went quiet and didn't seem to have too much of a desire to want to stick around. He just told me that he would sort out the car situation and that he would let me know when it was done.

I was obviously happy with that and let him know it, lying back on my pillow with my hands behind my head, letting him see that I was very satisfied with what had just taken place. Then he left, and while I had felt like taking a nap, I decided to take a shower, which is where I am now.

The water is almost as hot as the memory of what just happened in the bedroom, and I'm having fun recollecting it all. But that's nothing compared to how much fun it is when my mind drifts to thoughts of Lucy and how she is going to feel when she finds out what Ryan has done.

I imagine she'll be shocked, then upset, then angry, although that order might differ. One thing that is for sure is that I will be on hand to see how she reacts because I'll be the one to break the news to her. But I won't just do it by telling her what happened.

I'll be sure to show her too.

Ryan has no idea the true scope of what he has just done because he has no idea that my phone was recording the whole thing from its hiding place on the shelf in my bedroom. The footage it captured will be all the evidence I need to hurt Lucy and show her that when it comes to affairs of the heart, I have her beat there.

Let's see how much pride she takes in those other wins she has had over me when she sees what I have done with the man she loves.

I eventually leave the shower, and having wrapped my wet body in a thick towel, I return to the bedroom where I observe the crumpled bedsheets and the silk dressing gown strewn across the floor. My bedroom doesn't look like this very often because I don't make a habit of inviting guys over to my place, and I don't waste any time in tidying up, restoring the room to being neat and tidy before I sit down on the edge of the bed and watch the secret recording one more time.

The images are great, but it's the sound that really makes it.

Ryan's breathless panting as he moves his hands over my body really gives it an extra kick.

I can't wait to show Lucy this footage, and I think I know the perfect time to do it. She is due to give a big presentation tomorrow to a couple of external clients who are coming into the office to hear what she and Greg can offer them as they consider their options for their office renovation. It stands to be a six-figure contract if she can get it, and I know Lucy has been prepping hard to make sure she makes a good pitch, but there are some things she can't prepare for.

She won't be prepared for seeing the video of Ryan on top of me.

Showing her this video at any time will devastate her, but I might as well do it when I can hurt her in another way too. There'll be no way she can give a good presentation after having her heart broken seconds before walking into that boardroom. Hurting my rival both personally and professionally in one fell swoop is the kind of efficiency I strive for.

I spend the rest of the evening amusing myself by thinking about how Ryan will be behaving around Lucy now. He'll probably text her and tell her he's just had a quiet night and that there's nothing particular to report. Because of that, she will be content and without worry, totally oblivious to the truth as she settles down for a good night's rest ahead of her big day in the office tomorrow. But I find it difficult to sleep as I lie in the bed where Ryan lay only a few hours ago. I'm simply too excited for dawn to come and for me to walk into that office and see Lucy.

Like a child on Christmas Eve, I spend the night tossing and turning and watching the clock. By the time the sun comes up, I am already up too, dressing myself in my finest office attire because I want to not only feel good today but look good too.

Then, armed with a fierce determination and a mobile phone full of incriminating evidence, I walk out of the front door and get into my still slightly damaged car.

The dent in the front of it is a reminder of what I did to start this devious plot with Ryan.

But the hurt on Lucy's face when I show her the video will be the proof that I have just ended it.

36

LUCY

I've learnt how best to handle my nerves ahead of an important event over the years as I have aged and matured. Back when I was a teenager, I would stay up all night revising for an exam the following day, believing that the more hours I put in would give me more chance of a better result. I lost count of how many exams I sat while struggling to keep my eyes open because of that, not that I ever failed. Failure has never been an option for me, even from a young age. But as I got older, I started to realise that staying up all night was not the best way of maximising my potential, and getting a good night's sleep is one of the best things anybody can do to achieve peak performance.

That's why I went to sleep early last night, forgoing the alternative, which was to stay up into the early hours and keep going over the important presentation I have to make today.

The clients I will be pitching to today are already on the premises, currently sipping on a cup of coffee in Greg's office as he talks to them about a couple of things he wishes to discuss in private. But as soon as they are done in there then the conversation will move to the boardroom, and that is where I will come in, striding out in front of them all and standing in front of the large projector screen upon which will be the facts and figures

I am intending to use to get the clients to award us their project.

Things have gone very well for me since I started working here, but I am aware that today is a big test, and any mistake on my part could easily undo all the good work I have done so far. That's why I was up early this morning after a refreshing sleep, and after a coffee of my own, I delivered my presentation to the one person who has always been my harshest critic.

Kirsty sat patiently and listened intently as I presented to her, and even though she wouldn't have had a clue what I was talking about, she made sure to give me the best constructive criticism she could. She told me when I was talking too fast or dwelling too long on a particular slide. She noted if I was using too many hand gestures or not enough. And most importantly, she let me know if I sounded like a saleswoman who really believed in what they were selling.

Thankfully, I got a good review, even if it was a little biased coming from my best friend, and armed with the minor critiques Kirsty had, I have shaped and moulded this presentation into something I am convinced will deliver the result I need it to.

Now all I have to do is wait for Greg and the clients to enter the boardroom so I can get this over with.

I pace around in the corridor outside the boardroom as I wait for them to appear, reading through my notes one more time even though I know it all word for word at this stage. But I'm interrupted a moment later by the appearance of Jess, who smiles when she sees me and asks me if I am ready for what I am about to do.

'I think so,' I tell her before realising that answer doesn't make me sound as confident as I could be, so I correct it. 'Yeah, I've got this,' I add for clarity.

'Great. You'll be fine. I've done a few of these things myself. The trick is to break the ice early when you get in there. Make them laugh. Put them at ease. But I'm sure you know all of that anyway.'

'Yeah, but thank you,' I say, and I'm pleased that Jess is being helpful to me. She must know that if I nail this presentation and secure the contract then there's a good chance that I'll be scooping the big bonus again next month ahead of her. But she's gone out of her way to make sure I'm ready, and I admire her for that. I guess we don't have to be in competition 24/7, which is a relief because, frankly, it's more than a little exhausting.

But just before Jess walks away and leaves me to carry on rehearsing, she tells me that she has something funny to show me on her phone.

I'm not sure I really have time for looking at silly videos or memes that one of her friends might have sent her, but she already has her device out, and I guess it will only take a second. Plus a little laughter might help put my mind at ease too, so I guess it can't hurt.

'Here it is,' she says as she finds what she's looking for. 'What do you think of this?'

She turns her screen towards me, and I see a video, although I'm not sure at first what it's about. Then I see that there appears to be a man and a woman in bed together, and they're being quite passionate.

215

I let out a laugh just then, but more out of nervousness because this doesn't seem like the kind of thing that is appropriate to be shown in the workplace. But I'm guessing there is a punchline coming any second now, and I assume it's one of those TV adverts from another country where they can get away with riskier advertisements than we can do in the UK.

But that all changes when I see that Jess is the woman in the video.

'Is that you?' I ask her, really hoping I'm mistaken, and it's just someone who looks like her. But Jess doesn't answer me. She just waits for me to notice who she is with in the video, and when I do, I drop the papers in my hand on the floor in shock.

'What is this?' I cry. 'Is that Ryan?'

Jess shrugs as she continues to watch the video, and even though it's distressing for me to see it, I keep watching it too, but only to get absolute confirmation that it really features my boyfriend and the woman standing beside me. Once I am absolutely sure that is the case, I try and grab the phone, but Jess swipes it out of the way just in time before stepping back so I can't try and get it again.

'What the hell is that? What have you done?' I cry as the woman before me keeps smirking.

'What's wrong? You didn't think Ryan loved you, did you?'

'He's my boyfriend!'

'He's certainly not acting like that here, is he?'

'You bitch!'

I rush towards her to try and get the phone again, although I'd be just as happy with getting hold of a fistful of her hair at this point. But just before I can do either of those things, the door to Greg's office opens and he walks out, closely followed by the two clients who I am supposed to be presenting to any second now.

I stop immediately and do my best to disguise the fact that I am angry and upset while Jess quickly puts her phone away and does her best to look normal too.

'Hey, Lucy. I think we're ready for you now if you'd like to join us in the boardroom,' Greg says to me with a smile before leading the clients on to the next meeting place.

'Oh, okay, I'll be right there,' I manage to muster out as I wait for the three men to get further down the corridor before I turn back to Jess, rage still burning inside me.

But she's just smiling.

'Good luck in there,' she tells me. 'Something tells me you're going to need it.'

She walks away from me then, the phone with the disturbing evidence on it safely tucked away in her trouser pocket and leaving me to debate whether to go after her and demand some answers or go the other way to the boardroom where the clients are waiting for me to speak.

I really want to talk to Jess and demand some answers, as well as call Ryan and see what he has to say for himself, but I take a deep breath and tell myself that I can deal with those two later. Right now, it's time to focus on work. I can't mess this up, nor will I give Jess the satisfaction of seeing me doing so.

Come on, Lucy. You can do this. You can walk in there and present like a pro.

And you can forget about what you have just seen on that video.

Yeah, right.

I know I'm screwed before I even walk in there.

The next half an hour is just confirmation of that fact.

37

JESS

I don't even have to ask Lucy how her presentation went because I can see the disappointment on Greg's face as he leaves the boardroom and shows the two potential clients out. He doesn't look happy, and I suspect it's because Lucy has just made a mess of things and ruined any chances this company has of being awarded that expensive contract.

As I watch the three men walk away from my vantage point at my desk, I don't see Lucy come out. She must still be in there, probably trying to come to terms with the fact that she is no longer Greg's favourite.

I very much look forward to regaining that title.

But Lucy does emerge a few minutes later, and I wonder if she is going to march right over to me and pick up where she left off earlier, demanding answers as to how Ryan came to be in my bed and why. But she doesn't come towards me.

Instead, she goes straight in the direction of the HR office.

Fair enough. Lucy wants to play by the rules. She could have come over here and tried to push me off my chair, but she is going to keep things professional and air her grievances with the man who is tasked with making sure all employees behave appropriately in this office at all times.

I imagine that James, the HR manager, will be shocked to hear what Lucy is about to tell him, and it won't be long until he calls me into his office to join the conversation. But I was half-expecting this, so I'm not afraid of that. As always, I'm prepared for anything.

I see the door to the HR office close, and I wait patiently for it to open again, keeping myself occupied by responding to a couple of emails in my inbox and generally having a pleasant morning. But the door eventually opens again, and when it does, I was right.

James wants to see me.

'Is everything okay?' I ask him as I enter his office and see Lucy already seated by his desk.

'I'm not sure it is,' James admits as he closes the door and doublechecks to make sure it is definitely sealed because he really doesn't want any of this being overheard by another colleague out there. 'Lucy has made a very troubling accusation.'

'What's that?' I reply, pretending to be shocked.

'Oh, don't pretend like you don't know what I'm talking about!' Lucy cries as she gets up from her chair, but James makes sure to position himself in between us out of fear of there being any violence.

'Lucy, please,' he pleads. 'Give me a chance to explain to Jess what we have talked about.'

'She already knows what we have talked about! It's that video on her phone! The video of her with my boyfriend!'

I'm still making sure to look confused by what I'm hearing, and I look to James as if he can help me shed some light on what is going on here.

'Lucy has explained to me how you showed her a video,' James tells me. 'A rather graphic video, I might add. Is that true?'

'What?' I reply, still playing dumb.

'She's lying! Check her phone!' Lucy cries again, and she tries to get towards me to presumably find my device, but James takes another step in between us to keep us apart.

'What the hell are you talking about?' I ask to further reinforce my stance that I have absolutely no clue what all of this is about.

'Please, just check her phone. The video is on there!' Lucy urges James, and while I'm initially not sure if he will make such a request because my phone is my private property, he does see that that might be the only way to sort this out.

'Would you mind showing us what's on your phone?' he asks me tentatively, probably aware that I have the right to say no and drag this out a lot longer. But I don't do that. In fact, I'm happy to give them both what they want.

'Sure, I've got nothing to hide,' I say as I take out my phone and enter the pin code before holding it out for James to take.

The HR Manager begins to browse through my device while Lucy looks on, and now it's her turn to appear confused. She is obviously wondering why I would just give my device up so easily when it holds such incriminating evidence on me.

Unless…

'There's no video here,' James says as he keeps looking. 'I can't see anything like what you were referring to.'

He looks to Lucy who is still playing catch-up, but it doesn't take her too much longer to figure it out.

'She must have deleted it! Why else would she give you her phone?'

'What are you talking about? I haven't deleted anything because there was nothing to delete,' I say whilst rolling my eyes. 'Would somebody please explain to me what is going on now?'

James continues checking on the phone a little longer just to make sure, but he can look all he wants. That video is long gone because, as Lucy just guessed, I deleted it. There was no point in me keeping hold of it after all because I was the only one who could be damaged by doing such a thing. The damage was done once I had shown it to Lucy the first time, so it was hastily removed from my device after that.

'There's nothing here,' James determines after checking one final time, and he hands my phone back to me, which I accept with a shake of the head as if it was stupid for him to even have to check it in the first place.

'There was a video! You can't let her get away with this!'

'Get away with what?' I ask.

'Sleeping with my boyfriend!'

'Excuse me?'

'Stop denying it, whore!'

Lucy goes for me then, and James does well to stop her from lashing out at me as I step back and get away from her flailing arms.

'Are you going to let her get away with making crazy accusations like that?' I ask the exasperated HR Manager. 'And that name she just called me?'

'Look, I think everybody just needs to calm down for a second,' James tries, but that's never going to work, at least not for Lucy anyway.

'Why did you do this?' she demands to know. 'What have I ever done to you?'

'If that's all then can I leave now?' I ask James.

'No, not until I know you two aren't going to start a fight out in the office,' he tells us both.

'I'm not going to fight anybody,' I say with a simple shrug, but it takes Lucy a lot longer than that to convince him that she is not going to cause any more problems here today.

But eventually she concedes too, telling James that she won't do anything inappropriate in the office, and that's when he seems happier to let us leave.

'Maybe this is all a big misunderstanding,' he tells us. 'But whatever is going on between you two, may I remind you that any violence or abuse will not be tolerated in the workplace and will result in disciplinary action should it occur.'

With that warning still ringing in our ears, James opens his office door and allows the pair of us to leave. I decide to let Lucy go first, mainly because I don't want to turn my back to her in case she goes for me again. But there's no more drama as we leave the office, although that changes a little once James has closed his door and left us two alone.

'You bitch,' Lucy says to me under her breath so none of our colleagues can hear her. 'Why would you do this?'

But it's good that's she's being considerate of them, and I decide to do the same as I step closer to her to give her my answer.

'That's what you get for thinking you're better than me,' I tell her firmly. 'Let me make this clear. I don't lose at anything. Ever.'

'Oh my God, is this what it's all about?' Lucy says, looking mortified. 'Because I beat you in the challenges and got a bigger bonus than you? Is that it?'

But I don't even try to deny it or defend it. I just glare at Lucy before walking back to my desk, and while she doesn't follow me, I don't care.

She knows that I've won now.

I suspect she won't be bothering me again.

38

LUCY

It's times like these that a person needs a best friend, and thankfully, I have one who is on hand to help me through this difficult time.

'Red or white?' Kirsty asks me as she holds up two different coloured bottles of wine as we stand in the supermarket just around the corner from the bar we have spent the first half of this night in.

'Whatever,' I say with a grumpy shrug, and Kirsty decides that she will buy both just to be sure.

We leave the supermarket after paying for our drinks and begin the short walk to our flat, and even though I'm feeling a little more relaxed after a few beverages with my friend after work this evening, I'm still a long way from getting over what has happened to me. Kirsty can tell that, which is why she is continuing to remind me how much I need to try and forget about the two people who have betrayed me.

'They're not worth it,' she tells me as the bottles clink together in the plastic bag in her hand, but I ignore that comment and carry on talking about them.

'Maybe I should have expected something like this with Jess. I wanted to believe that we were friends, but there was always an edge there with her, and I guess we were just too similar. But I never thought Ryan would do something behind my back.'

'Men. They're all a waste of time,' Kirsty tells me, which goes against everything she was telling me when she wanted me to get a boyfriend, but never mind.

'I should phone him now and let him know what I think of him. Or better yet, I should go to his place and do it face to face.'

'No, that's a bad idea.'

'Why? He deserves all the names I'm going to call him.'

'I know he does, but you'll only make yourself upset too. Trust me, the best thing to do is to try and forget about them.'

'I can't forget about them though, can I? Ryan keeps ringing me wanting to know why I text him to say it's over, and I have to see Jess every day at work.'

You can ignore Ryan, and he'll get the hint eventually. But I admit Jess is more of a problem.'

'I'm going to have to quit my job.'

'No, don't do that!'

'I can't stay there and sit across from her every day!'

'But don't you see that's what she wants? She would love to get rid of you so she can go back to being the best salesperson on the team and getting the bigger bonuses. Don't give her that satisfaction.'

My friend makes a good point about how I shouldn't just make things easy for Jess by handing in my notice. But the thought of walking into that office tomorrow and seeing her is making me feel sick. It's not just what she did with Ryan, although that is bad enough. It's the reasoning she had for doing so. It was bone-chilling.

'I don't know if I even want to be around someone like her,' I admit as our flat comes into view. 'How sad and empty her life must be to choose competition over friendship.'

'She's obviously not a very happy person, and that's why she's done this,' Kirsty explains to me as she takes out her keys. 'She was bitter about what you had, and she ruined it. Now she thinks you're just as alone as she is, except you're not because you have me, and she has no one.'

'I suppose,' I say as I follow my friend into the building, and we plod up the staircase towards our front door. 'I still can't believe it though. To actually film it and then show me it. What kind of craziness is that?'

'It's insane,' Kirsty admits as we step inside, and she gets to work on fixing us both another drink.

I slump down on the sofa and let out a frustrated sigh as I wait for my wine to be delivered, and while I do, I check my phone again, seeing the missed calls and messages from Ryan. He wants an explanation as to why I no longer wish to see him, and I should probably tell him that I found out what he did with Jess, not only because he should know but because it might help me get some answers as to how she was able to find him and seduce him.

I have to assume she followed us and saw him. But who knows? That woman is obviously crazy enough to do anything.

'Here we go,' Kirsty says when she reappears with my glass of wine, and I smile weakly at her before she sits down beside me.

'Thanks,' I mutter before taking a sip and trying not to think about how much worse I might feel in the morning when I have a hangover to add to the equation.

'I think you should walk into that office tomorrow with your shoulders rolled back, and your head held high, and you let that bitch know that you are not beaten,' Kirsty tells me with a nod. 'You're a strong woman, and you can't let her keep you down.'

'That sounds easier said than done,' I reply, trying to imagine myself walking in full of confidence and bravado, but I just can't picture it. But Kirsty is not letting this pity party last any longer.

'You can do it,' she tells me firmly. 'You're the person who gets up early to go running while everyone else sleeps. You're the person who started a new job and got the highest sales in the first week. And you're the person who would never sleep with someone else's boyfriend just to spite them.'

I don't need my best friend to try and big me up, but it is quite nice to hear her remind me that I am a successful woman who has never stooped to the levels that my rival has.

'You're right,' I say, feeling emboldened by both my friend's words and the wine going into my system. 'I'm better than her, and I should prove it by sticking around and making things hard for her.'

'That's my girl!'

Kirsty clinks her glass against mine before going back into the kitchen to get the bottle she left in there because we're already in need of a refill. While she's gone, I check my phone again and decide that it is time to send a message to Ryan. But I'm no longer interested in getting his side of the story or trying to figure out how Jess got him into her bed. Frankly, I don't care because it doesn't matter. He is dead to me now, just like that woman is. And I let him know it by texting him to say that I feel like I can do better than him, so I'm going to have fun proving it. Then I leave it at that, aware that such a message will only drive Ryan even more crazy trying to figure it all out.

But now all my focus is on tomorrow morning when I will return to the office and sit down in my chair opposite the woman who has not only ruined my first serious relationship in a long time but also ruined my first big presentation at work.

She thinks she has struck the telling blow and that she has won.

But she is wrong.

It's time to show her what a real winner looks like.

39

JESS

I wasn't sure if Lucy would turn up for work today after what happened yesterday, but she is in the office, and she seems to be doing her best to make it look like recent events haven't bothered her. While she hasn't said a word to me, she has been chatting with a few of our other colleagues seated nearby, as well as making several phone calls to potential clients, so I guess she is trying to carry on as best she can. But I see through her façade, and I know that she will be suffering on the inside.

How can she not, sitting opposite the woman who slept with her boyfriend? But I want her to suffer, and I want her to ultimately leave this job and go and work somewhere else. I might have to be patient to get what I want, but I'm sure it's only a matter of time because I doubt that she can keep this act up forever. And right now, it's time for a big test of it because Greg has just called the sales team into a meeting.

I watch Lucy walk into the meeting room ahead of me and smirk at how she is trying to appear confident and composed by standing tall and puffing her chest out. But it's fake confidence, and I'm sure it won't take much to make it crumble. Here's hoping I get a chance to start chipping away at it over these next few minutes.

Greg starts the meeting by running through a few updates regarding certain projects we are bidding for, but it's all fairly bland stuff and not much I don't already know, so I'm only partially listening. It's funny how my attention span wanes when I'm in a meeting that isn't about bonuses. But Lucy seems a lot more engaged, and I watch her write down several things on her notepad, which is either because she is genuinely interested or she is just trying to look good in front of the boss. I suspect the latter because she will almost certainly have a lot of making up to do to Greg after what I presume was a disastrous showing on her part in that presentation.

'Jess? Anything to add?'

I realise Greg is talking to me then, and I really wish I knew what he wanted me to contribute to, but I don't have a clue.

'Erm...' I begin before I get cut off by Lucy, who decides to answer for me.

'I actually spoke to them this morning, and they have asked if I can go and meet with them on Friday,' Lucy tells Greg, who seems a little surprised by that but moves on. But I'm not ready to move on.

'Wait a minute. Who are you meeting on Friday?'

I want to make sure that Lucy wasn't just referring to a client that I am supposed to be handling then, but Greg confirms my worst fears.

'The McKenzie account. Are you even listening?'

'Yeah. Why is Lucy calling the client I'm in charge of?'

I'm expecting Greg to answer that, but Lucy does instead.

'I just felt like things could move a little faster there, so I thought I'd pick up the phone and see what I could do,' she says with a smile and a shrug, but the implication is clear. She is trying to make it sound like she can get things done that I can't.

'You have no right to do that,' I say, feeling myself losing control of my emotions, and I know this isn't the time or the place. But I can't help it. I thought I'd wounded Lucy and put her back in her place, yet here she is thinking she can potentially steal clients from me and claim those sales for herself?

'Lucy has a point. Things have been moving very slowly with that account,' Greg says, which doesn't help my cause. 'It's not like you at all, Jess, but you have seemed distracted lately. Any reason for that?'

I shake my head because I can hardly tell the truth and say that I've been too busy bedding my colleague's boyfriend to show her that I'm the better woman.

'I just don't think it's very professional, that's all,' I say, to which Lucy rolls her eyes, although Greg doesn't notice because he's already looking back down at his paper and looking to move on to the next topic. But just before he does, he makes sure to put Lucy in her place as well.

'Let's hope your meeting on Friday goes a lot better than your meeting yesterday,' he says in a clear reference to Lucy's botched presentation. I notice the hurt on Lucy's face after that comment and can't help but smile, which she sees and doesn't appreciate just as much as I don't appreciate her calling people who are supposed to be my clients.

The rest of the meeting passes by without as much tension, but as we all stand up to leave, Greg asks if Lucy and I will stay behind for a moment because he would like to speak to us in private.

'I'm not sure what's going on between you two, but I want you to know that I've noticed it, and it can't carry on if it's going to affect your performance here,' the boss says once everyone else has left.

'It's not affecting my performance,' I say quickly.

'Mine neither,' Lucy doesn't hesitate to add.

'You expect me to believe that?' Greg says, looking like he is doing his best to stay calm and knowing how passionate he can get about business matters, I'm not sure I want to see him lose his temper. 'Tell me your poor presentation yesterday wasn't down to whatever's going on between you, Lucy. And Jess, you've worked here for how long? And you have never moved slowly on an account, yet you've started to do so now?'

Both Lucy and I try and defend ourselves, but Greg cuts us off, not willing to hear any of it.

'James spoke to me earlier, and while he couldn't tell me the specific details, he did say that there may be something I need to sort out between you two soon. So, is there?'

Greg waits for an answer from either of us, but I say nothing, just like Lucy. Then we shake our heads to let our boss know everything is okay, which is laughable, but he doesn't need to know that.

'Okay, good. Now get back to work,' he tells us and opens the door for us to leave.

We leave the meeting room, and I'm heading back to my desk, but just before I get there, Lucy asks if she can have a word with me.

'What?' I ask as I stop walking.

'I just want you to know that this isn't over,' she says.

'Of course it isn't. I'm not going to stop until I've got you out of here.'

'Why can't you accept that I am better than you at certain things? Is your ego really that fragile that it won't let you lose at anything?'

'There's nothing wrong with my ego. I'm just a winner, and you got lucky. But your luck has run out now.'

'We'll see about that. It's the marathon next week, and I look forward to finishing ahead of you to prove to you once again that I am better.'

'That's funny, Ryan said I was better.'

I'm doing what I can to get a rise out of Lucy in the hopes that she might do something stupid like hit me so I can get her fired. But she keeps her composure and doesn't make it that easy for me.

'You're pathetic,' she says, shaking her head and heading back to her desk.

'Funny, I think the same about you,' I call after her before following her back to my own seat.

Nothing else is said between us for the rest of the day, but it doesn't need to be. We both know what the other is thinking, and more importantly, we both know what the other is going to do after work tonight.

We're going to be out running, training hard for the marathon so that we can beat the other one.

40

LUCY

I fidget with the black vest that hangs over my torso as I stand on the start line for the impending marathon, doing my best to try not to think too much about how far I'm going to have to run today. I've prepared extensively, but that still doesn't mean I'm not nervous as I stand with the other participants, all of them wearing their own bibs and sporting the number they were assigned by the race organisers. I don't know the exact number of people that have entered to run today, just that it's a big one, yet despite the large crowd around me, I have still managed to spot Jess.

I saw her when I arrived here. She was over by the benches, stretching her hamstrings and windmilling her arms, looking very much like she meant business. I don't think she has seen me, but I have made sure to keep my eye on her ever since I spotted her, and I can see her now, a dozen yards or so to my left, standing near the front and accepting the cup of water from one of the many volunteers helping out here.

She finishes the water and scrunches up the cup before tossing it into the large trash can by the side of the track that marks out the beginning of this long and winding route that runs all over town and back again, a daunting 26.2 miles in total. But I can't tell if Jess is looking tense or focused as I keep watching her go through a few more stretches before another organiser comes on the microphone and tells everybody to take their places.

This is it.

What all the training has led to.

Or rather, what all the fighting between Jess and I has led to.

I know she is fiercely determined to beat me here today, and her finishing in a quicker time than me does not bear thinking about. I can scarcely imagine the pleasure she will take in that. The way she will torment me at work. The grin on her face because she thinks she is better than me.

I can't allow it.

She cannot finish this marathon ahead of me.

'Runners, on your marks,' the official says, and everybody stops stretching, drinking or chatting and focuses on that command.

'Set…'

'GO!'

A loud crack of a race pistol complements the enthusiastic order, and with that, several hundred people start jogging at the same time.

I notice a few higher-level athletes who are already racing away, but I resist the urge to go off too quickly and stay in the middle of the pack because there's a long way to go, and the last thing I want to do is burn myself out.

It seems like Jess is following that same tactic, and she maintains a steady pace, a little ahead of me, but I'm happy to hang back for now and keep a visual on her, so I know what is required of me the further we go.

In time, this dense pack of runners will spread out, and there will be more chance for making tactical decisions then, but for now, we all move as one, passing the hundreds of cheering family members, friends and locals who have come out to lend their support.

I'm feeling good as I slip into a comfortable rhythm and start chipping away at all the miles ahead of me. I'm certainly feeling much better than the poor person who is attempting to run this marathon inside a giant chicken costume because they clearly didn't account for the temperature inside the huge outfit when they came up with the idea. But as the chicken sadly falls by the wayside, I keep going, and so does Jess, still ahead of me but by no means too far ahead for me to reel her in.

It's around the midpoint of the marathon that things really start to get challenging because we've all been running for around an hour and a half, and this is when aching muscles begin to feel even sorer, and any injuries carried over from training really begin to rear their ugly head. Fortunately, I'm relatively injury-free, so I am only having to do battle with the more general aches and pains that come with long-distance running, and I'm finding that it's more the mental side of things that is the most challenging now.

One foot in front of the other.

Just keep going.

You can do this.

The motivating mantras I am internally reaffirming to myself over and over again are doing enough to keep me moving, and while they might not win me any awards for inspiration, they see me to the sixteen-mile marker, and that's when I decide to shift gears.

Increasing my pace just enough to start closing the gap between Jess and I, I keep my eyes on the number on the back of her vest as I near her, and it's only when I'm alongside her that I decide to make my presence known.

'Keep up, dear,' I say before sprinting past Jess and leaving her trailing in my wake.

I smile to myself as I keep moving, and while I ease off the pace slightly, I don't slow down perhaps quite as much as I should, considering that there are still ten miles to go. That's because I am trying to spook Jess into going faster than she wants to do, and knowing her as well as I do, there is no way she will be content to stay behind me and risk the gap between us getting any bigger.

It's a gamble to change my own race pace to try and mess with Jess's, but I feel it's one worth taking, and I continue to push myself hard in the hope that Jess is now doing the same thing behind me.

Glancing over my shoulder a moment later reveals to me that she is indeed running as fast as I am, and not only that, but she is catching me up again.

Now the race is really on.

I keep going, but Jess is too quick for me at this point, and she regains the lead, not choosing to say anything as she passes, but she does make sure to give me a smile as she goes.

239

I grit my teeth and try and maintain my pace, but it's hard. I'm afraid I'm going way too fast considering where we are in the marathon, but I can't let Jess slip from view.

'Come on, keep going,' I say to myself, and the fact that the positive affirmations have been upgraded from internal words to ones I speak out loud is further proof that this situation is getting more serious.

The next three miles pass by in a blur, and while I'm glad to get them over with quickly, I'm still aware that this pace is surely an unsustainable one. But Jess keeps glancing over her shoulder, and as long as she sees me on her tail, I know she isn't going to ease up.

I'm starting to wonder just how long she can keep going at this speed, but it's around the twenty-mile mark when I see her stumble slightly before her legs definitely begin to wobble, and she struggles to keep her balance.

Many runners refer to 'The Wall' when taking part in an event like this. It's that part of the race where the body hits its limit, and there's only two options then.

Fight through it no matter how hard it gets.

Or give up.

Is that what's happening to Jess? Has she hit the wall right here?

If she has then she has gone into it headfirst because not only is she wobbling now, but she is actually falling over.

I hear several loud gasps from the crowd as participant number 576 hits the tarmac, and while none of the other runners around Jess stop to see if they can help her, I decide that I have to stop, if only to see if my rival is really down and out or if she still has it in her to get back to her feet and carry on with the race.

But it's clear when I reach her that Jess's marathon is over.

That's because not only is she lying on the ground, but her eyes are closed, and she isn't moving.

Somebody in the crowd sees that Jess is in serious trouble if the loud scream I hear is anything to go by, but I'm less emotional than that person. That could be because I'm severely out of breath and still recovering from the punishing pace Jess and I were setting, or it could be because it's quite nice to see my foe on the ground in such a bad state.

A passive observer might call me heartless, but I can't help the smile that spreads across my face as I look down at Jess lying by my feet.

But then I snap back into action when I see a couple of paramedics running towards me, and I know that as bad as things have got between me and my old friend, I still don't want her to die.

'Jess? Can you hear me?' I call out as I crouch down beside the fallen runner and try to stir her back to consciousness.

But there is no response, and it's clear this is something only a medical expert can sort out now, so I step back as the help arrives and watch the paramedics get to work.

I guess neither Jess nor I will be finishing this marathon today.

But some things are more important than who comes first or second.

Like the difference between life and death, for example.

41

The first thing I see when I open my eyes is a beautiful bunch of flowers. The second thing I see is a cheap plastic chair that looks similar to the ones in some of the old offices that I help to renovate. But it's the third thing I see that causes me to sit up in the bed and frown.

There's somebody holding the flowers, and they are sitting in the chair next to my bed.

It's Lucy.

And she is smiling.

'Hey, good to have you back with us,' she says to me as she puts the flowers down and picks up a plastic cup of water before holding it out to me. 'Here, have a sip of this. You're probably dehydrated.'

I'm not sure where I am and why the woman I hate is trying to give me some water, but as I look around the room a little more, I figure out what is going on here.

I'm in hospital.

But why?

'What happened?' I ask as Lucy continues to hold the cup out in front of me.

'Don't you remember? You collapsed during the marathon.'

'What!'

'Yeah, you were just ahead of me, and you fell over. It was lucky the paramedics were quick to get to

243

you. But I've spoken to the doctor, and he tells me you are going to be just fine.'

I try my best to remember that, but I'm struggling. The last thing I recall was me running. Then I woke up here.

'What happened to me?' I ask.

'I guess you hit the wall,' Lucy replies. 'Hard.'

'I really don't remember.'

'It doesn't matter. The main thing is you're alright.'

There's a lot that is confusing me about this situation, but perhaps the main thing is that Lucy is being so nice to me. As far as I can remember, we hate each other's guts. So what's changed?

'Why are you here?' I ask her as I finally take the cup of water and alleviate my parched throat.

'I just figured it would be nice if somebody was here when you woke up, and the doctors didn't know who else to call. Plus, I was with you when it happened.'

I'd rather not dwell on the fact that the hospital staff would have had a hard time trying to find a loved one to contact who would have come rushing to be by my bedside because there is no one. But I also stop short of thanking Lucy for being here because I'm still confused about all of this.

'We didn't finish the race?' I ask as if that is the most important thing.

'No, we didn't,' Lucy says with a chuckle. 'But I'd say that's not very important right now.'

I finish the water and put the cup down on the bedside table beside the flowers, which Lucy must see me looking at because she comments on them then.

'I got those from a shop in this hospital,' she tells me. 'I figured they would be something nice for you to see when you woke up. Nicer than seeing me, anyway.'

I don't thank Lucy for the flowers, but I do smile at her comment.

'I'm not sure I could have brought myself to visit you if you had collapsed during the marathon,' I admit rather honestly, but Lucy doesn't seem hurt by that.

'I'm shocked,' she says, trying to keep a straight face, but she doesn't manage it, and both of us end up laughing.

'How far did we get?' I ask as I sit up in the bed and gingerly put a hand to my aching head.

'Twenty miles, so not too bad.'

'Damn it, we were so close.'

'If you think six miles is close then yeah, I guess we were.'

I laugh again, and despite everything that has happened between us, it's clear something has changed. And then my bitter rival confirms it.

'How about we call a truce?' Lucy suggests.

'A truce? Are you serious? After what I did with Ryan?'

'I'll admit that was the ultimate bitch move, but look what happened. You could have died during that marathon because you were trying so hard to beat me. Nothing's worth that.'

'I guess.'

'I mean, we both like to win, but if it's a choice between winning and dying, and losing and living, I know which one I'd rather choose.'

I can't argue with that, and as Lucy holds out her hand towards me, I feel compelled to shake it.

'Call it a draw?' Lucy asks me as we hold hands.

'Sure,' I reply with a shrug.

'Okay, well I better get going because I'm sure the doctor wants to talk to you. But I guess if everything is alright then I'll see you at work, yeah?'

'I guess you will.'

Lucy stands up, and I watch her heading for the door but before she goes, I have one last thing to say.

'Hey,' I call out, and she turns back from the doorway.

'What?'

'Thank you.'

Lucy smiles then makes her exit, and I'm left alone for a moment to stare at the wall opposite my bed and wonder how long I have to spend in here before I can go home. But I don't have to wait too long to possibly find that out because the door to my room opens again a moment later, and a man in a white coat walks in holding a clipboard.

'Hi, Jess. I'm Doctor Peckman. How are you doing?'

'Erm, yeah. I'm okay, I guess.'

'That's good. Do you mind if I take a seat?'

The doctor heads for the plastic chair next to me, and I shuffle myself up a little more in the bed in anticipation of the news I expect I am about to be given. Lucy told me that I collapsed, but I'm expecting a more precise diagnosis from the medical professional now in the room with me.

'Okay, so we've run some tests to see if we could find out what exactly caused your episode during the marathon,' Doctor Peckman begins, and I nod my head to show that I am following him so far. 'And that's where we found a troubling result.'

'What is it?'

The doctor lets out a deep sigh as he stares at the notes on his clipboard before looking me in the eyes and giving me the news.

'We found traces of Gamma Hydroxybutyrate in your system.'

'What's that?'

'It's more commonly known as the date rape drug.'

'What?'

'It seems you were drugged.'

'What the hell are you talking about?'

'Do you remember feeling drowsy before you collapsed?'

'No, I was actually feeling great, I think.'

'These drugs can induce a euphoric feeling.'

'I thought it was just all the adrenaline from running.'

'Unfortunately not.'

I try to process what I'm hearing, but it's almost too crazy to fathom.

'Can you think of anything that happened to you just before the race started?' Doctor Peckman asks.

'Like what?'

'Did anybody give you something to drink?'

I think back to before the marathon, but I can't recall anything like that.

'I don't think so. Maybe.'

'Okay, well you don't have to try and remember right now. But the police have been notified, and they would like to speak to you, when you are feeling better of course.'

'The police?'

'Yes. This is obviously a serious event. Somebody drugged you, and things could have gone a lot worse. Some people supplied with this drug end up in a coma, and it has even led to death in some cases.'

I'm horrified at what I'm hearing, but Doctor Peckman doesn't stop there.

'The fact is that unless you did this to yourself, which I'm sure you didn't, then somebody drugged you. Do you have any idea who that person might be?'

I laugh off the suggestion because it seems so ludicrous, but after those first few seconds of blissful ignorance pass, there is one person that comes to mind, and the flowers lying beside my bed are the reminder that she was here only a moment ago.

But no.

It couldn't be her.

Could it?

EPILOGUE

LUCY

I walk past dozens of parked vehicles in the hospital car park before I find my own and hop in behind the steering wheel. This is the car that I have just treated myself to with the proceeds from my first bonus from Greg, and while I'm by no means a petrolhead, this vehicle is considered a good performer, especially in the speed stakes. But I'm not doing any speeding as I drive away, passing a few patients in dressing gowns by the front door as well as a couple of paramedics getting into a parked ambulance before I leave the hospital grounds and get out onto the main road.

I wind down the window to get a little fresh air on my face as I cruise through town, all the while thinking about the patient I have just been to visit. I'm sure Jess appreciated the gesture, as well as the flowers, although I wonder how long it will be until she realises I haven't been operating with the best of intentions in our dealings lately.

Okay, I admit it.

I drugged her so that she wouldn't beat me in the marathon.

It obviously worked because she collapsed well short of the finish line, and overall, the whole thing was a success because while she lost consciousness, she has woken up and is expected to make a full recovery, which is good because I didn't want her to suffer any long-lasting effects.

I'm not a monster, after all.

I am a winner, however, and once Jess figures out what I did, she will see that too. I also doubt she will ever feel like trying to compete with me again now she knows what I am truly capable of. But that's for her to think about at a later date. Right now, I imagine she is just having a hard enough time trying to remember anything at all.

The drug I was able to successfully slip into her system was called GHB, and I deployed a very clever way of administering it. Knowing that all marathons are manned by numerous volunteers whose task it is to hand out cups of water to the runners, all I had to do was enlist the help of my very own volunteer to pretend to be no different to all the other helpers in their white t-shirts.

Kirsty was the 'fake volunteer', and she handed the spiked cup of water to Jess before the race began, just after I had pointed my rival out in the crowd so my friend could find her. I'm extremely grateful for the assistance of my best friend and flatmate, but considering what Jess did to me with Ryan, Kirsty was only too happy to help. Of course, I didn't mention to her that there was a slight risk Jess could die because I'm sure she wouldn't have been quite so keen to participate in my plan then, but those odds were small, and Jess has lived to tell the tale, so it's all good in the end.

Will Jess figure out that it was the volunteer that drugged her? I doubt it. One of the many consequences of consuming a drug like GHB is that the victim suffers memory loss, so she's unlikely to ever fully remember the day in question. It just remains to be seen whether she is smart enough to know it was me who masterminded the whole thing somehow.

I bring my vehicle to a stop at a red light and tap on the steering wheel in time to the music that is playing on my radio. It's been a rough few weeks with everything that has happened with Ryan and Jess, but I'm starting to feel like I am getting back to my old self again. I doubt I'll ever forgive myself for letting my standards slip and losing my disciplined edge by falling for some guy who turned out to be just as much of a waste of time as every other guy I've ever known. I really don't know what I was thinking when I decided to enter into a relationship with him. But that's the last time I make such a mistake. From now on, I'm back to the old me, the razor-sharp, super-focused, and ultra-competitive me that doesn't let others get the better of them and who wins at whatever she chooses to do.

As I wait for the red light to turn green, I glance to my left and look at the driver in the vehicle next to me. It's a guy of around twenty-five, and he seems to be bopping along to whatever is blasting out of his speakers too. But he notices me looking and gives me a smile, probably wondering if I'm attracted to him and eager to find out if I'm going to return the expression.

But I don't do that. Instead, I press my foot down on the accelerator, and while the handbrake is still on, the engine revs loudly, and the sound lets my fellow road user know that I'm interested in a little race once the traffic lights change colour.

Will he want to participate?

I certainly hope so.

But there will only be one outcome if he does.

Just like Jess, he will learn that it's not so easy to beat me.

However, I hope he still tries.

After all, it's the taking part that counts, right?

Download My Free Book

If you would like to receive a FREE copy of my psychological thriller 'Just One Second', then you can find the link to the book at my website www.danielhurstbooks.com

Thank you for reading *The Rivals*. If you have enjoyed this psychological thriller, then you'll be pleased to know that I have several more stories in this genre, and you can find a list of my titles on the next page. These include my bestselling book *Til Death Do Us Part*, which has a twist that very few people have been able to predict so far, and *The Passenger*, which became the number 1 selling psychological thriller in the UK in October 2021.

ALSO BY DANIEL HURST

TIL DEATH DO US PART
THE PASSENGER
THE COUPLE AT TABLE SIX
WE USED TO LIVE HERE
THE BREAK
THE RIVALS
WE TELL NO ONE
THE WOMAN AT THE DOOR
HE WAS A LIAR
THE BROKEN VOWS
THE WRONG WOMAN
THE TUTOR
THE NEIGHBOURS
RUN AWAY WITH ME
THE ROLE MODEL
NO TIME TO BE ALONE
THE BOYFRIEND
THE PROMOTION
THE NEW FRIENDS
THE BREAK
THE ACCIDENT

(All books available now on Amazon and Kindle Unlimited – read on to learn a little more about a few of them…)

TIL DEATH DO US PART

What if your husband was your worst enemy?

Megan thinks that she has the perfect husband and the perfect life. Craig works all day so that she doesn't have to, leaving her free to relax in their beautiful and secluded country home. But when she starts to long for friends and purpose again, Megan applies for a job in London, much to her husband's disappointment. She thinks he is upset because she is unhappy. But she has no idea.

When Megan secretly attends an interview and meets a recruiter for a drink, Craig decides it is time to act. Locking her away in their home, Megan realises that her husband never had her best interests at heart. Worse, they didn't meet by accident. Craig has been planning it all from the start.

As Megan is kept shut away from the world with only somebody else's diary for company, she starts to uncover the lies, the secrets, and the fact that she isn't actually Craig's first wife after all...

THE PASSENGER

She takes the same train every day. But this is a journey she will never forget...

Amanda is a hardworking single mum, focused on her job and her daughter, Louise. But it's also time she did something for herself, and after saving for years, she is now close to quitting her dreary 9-5 and following her dream.

But then, on her usual commute home from London to Brighton, she meets a charming stranger – a man who seems to know everything about her. Then he delivers an ultimatum. She needs to give him the code to her safe where she keeps her savings before they reach Brighton – or she will never see Louise again.

Amanda is horrified, but while she knows the threat is real, she can't give him the code. That's because the safe contains something other than her money. It holds a secret. *A secret so terrible it will destroy both her's and her daughter's life if it ever gets out...*

THE WRONG WOMAN

What if you were the perfect person to get revenge?

Simone used to be the woman other women would use if they suspected their partner was cheating. She would investigate, find out the truth and if the men were guilty, exact revenge in one form or another. But after things went wrong with one particular couple, Simone was forced to go into hiding to evade the law.

Having assumed a new identity, Simone is now Mary, a mild-mannered woman who doesn't raise her voice or get angry, meaning nobody would ever suspect her of being capable of the things she used to do for a living. But when she finds out that her new boyfriend is having an affair, it awakens in her the person she used to be. Plotting revenge, Mary reverts back to the woman she once was before she went on the run and became domesticated. That means Simone is back, and it also means that her boyfriend and his mistress are in for the shock of their lives.

They messed with her. *But they picked the wrong woman.*

259

THE WOMAN AT THE DOOR

It was a perfect Saturday night. *Until she knocked on the door...*

Rebecca and Sam are happily married and enjoying a typical Saturday night until a knock at the door changes everything. There's a woman outside, and she has something to say. Something that will change the happy couple's relationship forever...

With their marriage thrown into turmoil, Rebecca no longer knows who to trust, while Sam is determined to find out who that woman was and why she came to their house. But the problem is that he doesn't know who she is and why she has targeted them.

Desperate to save his marriage, Sam is willing to do anything to find the truth, even if it means breaking the law. But as time goes by and things only seem to get worse, it looks like he could lose Rebecca forever.

THE NEIGHBOURS

It seemed like the perfect house on the perfect street. *Until they met the neighbours...*

Happily married couple, Katie and Sean, have plenty to look forward to as they move into their new home and plan for the future. But then they meet two of their new neighbours, and everything on their quiet street suddenly doesn't seem as desirable as it did before.

Having been warned about the other neighbours and their adulterous and criminal ways, Katie and Sean realise that they are going to have to be on their guard if they want to make their time here a happy one.

But some of the other neighbours seem so nice, and that's why they choose to ignore the warning and get friendly with the rest of the people on the street. *And that is why their marriage will never be the same again...*

THE TUTOR

What if you invited danger into your home?

Amy is a loving wife and mother to her husband, Nick, and her two children, Michael and Bella. It's that dedication to her family that causes her to seek help for her teenage son when it becomes apparent that he is going to fail his end of school exams.

Enlisting the help of a professional tutor, Amy is certain that she is doing the best thing for her son and, indeed, her family. But when she discovers that there is more to this tutor than meets the eye, it is already too late.

With the rest of her family enamoured by the tutor, Amy is the only one who can see that there is something not quite right about her. But as the tutor becomes more involved in Amy's family, it's not just the present that is threatened. Secrets from the past are exposed too, and by the time everything is out in the open, Amy isn't just worried about her son and his exams anymore. She is worried for the survival of her entire family.

HE WAS A LIAR

What if you never really knew the man you loved?

Sarah is in a loving relationship with Paul, a seemingly perfect man who she is hoping to marry and start a family with one day, until his sudden death sends her into a world of pain.

Trying to come to terms with her loss, Sarah finds comfort in going through some of Paul's old things, including his laptop and his emails. But after finding something troubling, Sarah begins to learn things about Paul that she never knew before, and it turns out he wasn't as perfect as she thought. But as she unravels more about his secretive past, she ends up not only learning things that break her heart, but things that the police will be interested to know too.

Sarah can't believe what she has discovered. But it's only when she keeps digging that she realises it's not just her late boyfriend's secrets that are contained on the laptop. Other people's secrets are too, and they aren't dead, which means they will do anything to protect them.

RUN AWAY WITH ME

What if your partner was wanted by the police?

Laura is feeling content with her life. She is married, she has a good home, and she is due to give birth to her first child any day now. But her perfect world is shattered when her husband comes home flustered and afraid. He's made a terrible mistake. He's done a bad thing. *And now the police are going to be looking for him.*

There's only one way out of this. He wants to run. *But he won't go without his wife...*

Laura knows it is wrong. She knows they should stay and face the music. But she doesn't want to lose her man. She can't raise this baby alone. *So she agrees to go with him.* But life on the run is stressful and unpredictable, and as time goes by, Laura worries she has made a terrible mistake. They should never have ran. But it's too late for that now. Her life is ruined. The only question is: *how will it end?*

THE ROLE MODEL

She raised her. Now she must help her…

Heather is a single mum who has always done what's best for her daughter, Chloe. From childhood up to the age of seventeen, Chloe has been no trouble. That is until one night when she calls her mother with some shocking news. There's been an accident. *And now there's a dead body…*

As always, Heather puts her daughter's safety before all else, but this might be one time when she goes too far. Instead of calling the emergency services, Heather hides the body, saving her daughter from police interviews and public outcry.

But as she well knows, everything she does has an impact on her child's behaviour, and as time goes on and the pair struggle to keep their sordid secret hidden, Heather begins to think that she hasn't been such a good mum after all. *In fact, she might have been the worst role model ever…*

THE BROKEN VOWS

He broke his word to her. Now she wants revenge...

Alison is happily married to Graham, or at least she is until she finds out that he has been cheating on her. Graham has broken the vows he made on his wedding day. How could he do it? It takes Alison a while to figure it out, but at least she has time on her side. *Only that is where she is wrong.*

A devastating diagnosis means the clock is ticking down on her life now, and if she wants revenge on her cheating partner, then she is going to have to act fast. Alison does just that, implementing a dangerous and deadly plan, and it's one that will have far reaching consequences for several people, including her clueless husband.

INFLUENCE

Would you kill for a million followers?

Emily Bennett dreams of being a social media influencer, just like her idols, Mason Manor & Ivy Lane. But shortly after Ivy's untimely death, she is contacted by a secretive businessman who offers her the chance at the fame and fortune she so desperately craves.

While Emily initially gets to experience the things she has always wanted, it soon becomes clear that her new employer had sinister motives for approaching her, and it isn't long before she discovers that the life of her dreams comes with the kind of conditions that are the stuff of nightmares.

Social media isn't life or death.

It's more important than that.

THE 20 MINUTES SERIES

An original psychological thriller series showing how we are all more connected to each other than we think.

About The Author

Daniel Hurst lives in the Northwest of England with his wife, Harriet, and considers himself extremely fortunate to be able to write stories every day for his readers.

You can visit him at his online home
www.danielhurstbooks.com

You can connect with Daniel on Facebook at www.facebook.com/danielhurstbooks or on Instagram at www.instagram.com/danielhurstbooks

He is always happy to receive emails from readers at daniel@danielhurstbooks.com and replies to every single one.

Thank you for reading.

Daniel

Made in United States
North Haven, CT
13 April 2024

51262388R00161